MW01181991

In

Madison

An
Inspirational
Suspense Novel

By

Jane Priest Wilson

♡Jane Priest Wilson♡

To Nancy, with Love in Jesus!
God bless you -

Dedication

Above all, first and foremost, I dedicate this work of inspirational fiction to my Lord and Savior Jesus Christ, and I pray that He will be glorified in every way. It is to Him that I give this work and it is my earnest prayer that people will come to know Him through its message.

Secondly I sincerely dedicate this novel to my high school sweetheart. I express my deep love and appreciation to my precious husband, John, for his faithful, loving support. Without his witty ideas and encouragement, this work would not have ever happened or been published! He truly is my "best half"!

This novel is also dedicated to long-time family friend, Roy McGaa, who read my first draft when it was only a few chapters long. He looked at me in shock and said, "Do you mean to tell me it's *not* finished?" I promised him that I would dedicate it to him if I ever finished it! No, it wasn't finished then, but now, many years later it is finally ready for publication.

Jane Priest Wilson (August 2012)

Table of Contents

Acknowledgements

To my family members who supported me during the long process of writing, editing and completing the work, I sincerely give my heartfelt gratitude. Thank you, especially those of you who read, typed and edited this work. Special thanks to my granddaughter, Rebecca, who, at the age of eleven capably helped with typing this final draft, and to her sister Sarah who cheered her on! Also, I am very grateful to our son, Jimmy who provided me with a laptop! It is a far cry from the manual typewriter on which I originally wrote this book.

Grateful appreciation also goes to Jeremy Humphrey for his technical support. What a blessing! Thank you, to other friends, who stayed up all night to read my early manuscripts, which were typed on a manual typewriter, (as we had no electricity in those days, living in the north-woods). They all said, "I just had to find out what happened!" The encouragement of my Lord and all these different people surely made this work happen, and to them I will always be grateful.

Sincerely, Jane Priest Wilson (August 2012)

Miracle in Madison

Chapter 1

Far away in the forest the big man furtively maneuvered among the trees. He had a sinister way about him as he made his plans, constantly looking from side to side, then behind him as well. His feet shuffled through the leaves that had begun to fall to the forest floor. His mind was filled with the intent of his heart and he determined to do whatever it took to make his plan work…. anything… yes, *anything*. He tugged his hat lower on his forehead as he doggedly pushed his way through the brush.

***

Susan Greyson had been very happy that day in the early fall of 1978. Tragedy was impending, and she would have done things differently if she had only known. The water was crystal clear and ice cold. The fish swimming against the current made a silvery reflection. The morning air was fresh and clean, and the gentle breeze rustled the forest leaves.

These are probably the happiest days of my life, she thought, drawing her knees up to her chin. She gazed into the sparkling mountain stream, absorbing the beauty around her. Every sound was like music to her ears. She could hear birds singing playfully to each other. Above their song, she could hear the chattering of two red squirrels fussing over a nut. When Susan looked, she found the smallest one had a beautiful, bushy tail, and the other had a merry twinkle in his eyes. There was a raccoon across the stream peeking around a bush at her.

Susan wondered if they thought she was a part of the mountain scenery, because she had been sitting beside the stream for so long. She never lost that awe she felt toward the beautiful miracle of creation.

1

Her hands felt cool against her face as she brushed a tuft of hair away. She was a small woman, wearing blue jeans and a sweatshirt. The cool mountain air brought a glow to her fair skin, and her long dark hair swirled around her face in the breeze.

She was not alone. She could feel his presence through the sound of his axe against wood. She visualized him there beside the cabin, swinging his powerful arms, over and over. She had watched him at that chore so many times and had memorized each pulsating muscle in his strong back and arms. He would be pushing his damp, wayward black hair off his moist forehead. With every downward thrust, the crunch of steel against wood made a smacking echo in the woods. Susan smiled.

It would not be long until time to go in and make a batch of sourdough biscuits and some fresh milk gravy for breakfast. She knew he would be ravenous by the time he was finished.

She had learned to make sourdough long before coming here. It was more of a game to try out new recipes then. Now it made a lot of difference to them to have fresh hot bread at a meal. She was exuberant, sitting there on the big mossy rock. She took regular walks up here, and they always made her feel wonderful. She could hear the children laughing. Their happy voices nurtured her contentment.

***

Sometimes, she missed her friends from their old life, but never once had she regretted leaving. She had grown up in a large city and had always yearned to live in the country and be around animals. When she met Bob, and they had such similar desires, it seemed as if they were destined to achieve their goals.

One of those was to have two children to complete their family. They had one boy's name and one girl's name chosen long before their wedding day. It had seemed like an answered prayer when their children were born: first beautiful black-haired June and two years later darling black-haired Randy. They gave the pre-chosen names to their children; it would have been like a broken vow to name them otherwise.

Now they were living their most precious dream. They had wanted to be close to nature and raise their children in the woods. They sought to find peace and-tranquility away from the harsh realities of city life. Their deepest desire was to teach the children the values of life; the exquisite happiness in simplicity, the enrichment of learning to earn the things they wanted, the joy of watching new-born animals in the wild, and seeing those animal parents love and protect their babies. These things and many more could be gained by "living in the wilderness". Bob and Susan wanted their children to learn about the "birds and bees" by relating to natural things instead of reading about it or learning from the distorted whispers of other children.

It was after they came here that life found real meaning. There was that one very special event had changed everything! After that, at long last, they had found the peace and tranquility they had sought after so intensely.

**

Susan looked down the hill from where the laughter was coming. She could see her son, Randy and his twin friends, Kelly and Kenny Martin. They spent endless hours together. She grinned as she watched them running, shoving one another. One would stop and pick up a slick rock and sling it swiftly out over the cold water in the stream, making it skip across. Another would follow suit to see who could do the best. The brothers' blonde hair gleamed in the morning sun. Their happy voices were as musical as the forest sounds she had been so aware of only moments before.

"Mom, can we go fishing? We promise to bring you some fish for lunch! Please, Mama! Can we?" Randy always became excited when they went fishing, and Susan rarely refused him.

Before they had come here to live, he had never owned a fishing pole, and had been fishing only once with a Boy Scout Troop. Susan thought how grand it was that they had finally left the city and come to this wonderful, clean place. When Bob's great Uncle Richard had died they had no idea how it would change their lives. Bob and his uncle had never been close, but Bob's father had been Richard's favorite nephew, and since he was not living, the money was left to Bob as a tribute to his father.

The inheritance had been fairly small, in comparison to the size of the estate. Fortunately, it was just what Bob and Susan had been dreaming of and saving for. The unexpected income gave them enough to pay their debts and, combined with their savings, they paid cash for their little piece of land. They had no trouble selling their house in the city, so they had plenty of money for the move and to pay their living expenses while building the log cabin.

They truly believed that they would have made the move eventually, but the inheritance simply made it sooner. They had already planned on the area where they would move. They had visited it quite by accident when they were vacationing a year before. It was just what they had wanted, and all they had to do when they got the money was to go back and decide which piece of land to buy.

After the move, Bob got a job at a local sawmill, and they began their new life-style. For several weeks, Bob worked in exchange for lumber supplies he needed for the cabin. Then, after it was completed, he began to work for salary. He was thankful he truly enjoyed his job there.

The little town of Madison was like something out of a storybook. There was a little white church with a bell in the steeple. They could hear it ring every Sunday morning, even where they lived. It rang suddenly at times to alert the town to a crisis or important meeting.

There was a little grocery store, which always had just about everything you could need, plus some. Tom and Mary Martin, the twin's parents, ran the store together, and it was quite a family thing. Their home was right next-door.

Susan fell in love with that place the first time they visited Madison. The little white house was connected to the store by a stone room where they kept extra supplies. Honeysuckle and English Ivy clung to the walls of the structure. The emerald green grass was kept closely clipped and the borders were lined with brightly colored flowers.

There was an old-fashioned stone water well with a little, sloped roof. That day its shingles were still wet from an afternoon shower. Pumping the handle on the wooden cover, Susan drank deeply while the fragrances filled her head. She had loved Madison immediately, and that first impression still made her smile when she remembered. There was something other than charm that had attracted Susan. She couldn't quite put her finger on it at the time, but that Martin couple seemed very special the very first time she met them in the store.

The small town had only a few curving streets. Driving through, they noticed that the elementary school and high school were both in the same building. Even it was quaint with lots of ivy and neatly kept grass. There was one mammoth oak tree standing as a guardian.

All their married life they had made plans to be where they were now. They spent many hours talking and dreaming of the life they would have. They had learned all they could about gardening and canning. They had purchased all kinds of books to learn everything needed to live self -sufficiently, if necessary. It had not become necessary, but at least they were satisfied in the knowledge that they could survive. A lot of things they had learned from their books did help to make their "back to nature" lives more comfortable. The books were lined neatly on the shelves Bob had made. Neither of them were scholars, but both loved to read and thoroughly enjoyed their books, as did the children. Their books were read until the pages were creased and worn.

***

"Mommm!" Her son's anxious voice brought her back from her musings. She jumped up with a smile.

"Alright, Randy, but you must come to the cabin and let me fix you all some sandwiches. You haven't even had breakfast, you know." Susan knew how much her little family would enjoy a plate of fresh mountain trout for lunch. She agreed immediately to let him go.

It was almost fall and the pine needles made a carpet on the forest floor. As she walked down the hill toward their cabin, she breathed deeply and was exhilarated by the freshness of the pine scented mountain air. She had known how wonderful pine scent was, and now every breath was full and she was gloriously happy. When they made the move to the mountain, she had thrown away her cans of pine scent bought at the five and dime. She could remember how exuberant she felt that day, knowing she would have that fresh, natural scent with her always here on the mountain.

She threw her head back, taking a deep breath, and noticed how blue the sky was today. She felt sheltered by the covering of the blessed blue sky. She had never been so aware of it in the city. Surely God must have thought of her when He made that sky.

Soon, the log cabin came into view, and the pine trees towered above it, making it appear to be a miniature. It had been another dream come true for them, and building it had been one of the most satisfying experiences they had ever had. They used the best of both worlds, enjoying indoor plumbing, electricity, a gas heater, as well as the more old-fashioned wood cook stove and other items. They had made many mistakes as they went along, but laughingly declared that the next cabin would be a lot easier to build.

***

Of course, the three boys had raced to the cabin and were already waiting for Susan. They went around to the side, where Randy's daddy was still splitting firewood. He immediately put the boys to work stacking the wood, which they made into a game with an assembly line motion. Soon they had it all stacked. The three boys stood with their hands behind their backs, tapping their feet impatiently as if Bob was not working fast enough. They tried, without success, to conceal the grins on their young faces.

"You roughnecks better git into the house and eat if you wanna go fishin'!" He chuckled as he watched them grab up their fishing poles and scoot around to the front of the cabin.

Susan had gone into their cozy home, and as she entered, she had that familiar special feeling that the cabin always gave her. This place symbolized the culmination of their lifetime of dreams. Things that had happened in their little cabin had changed their lives forever.

As she bustled around the kitchen, the three boys helped themselves to the steaming mugs of cocoa that she had placed on the bar dividing the kitchen from the living area. They chattered excitedly about their plans for the day.

"Let's go down to the wide spot in the river and try for that old big monster, whaddya say?" Kenny's blue eyes flashed with anticipation. He always wanted to go to that particular spot, and two out of three times they did. It was their favorite swimming hole in the warm days of summer. In fact, that was where the twins and Randy had met.

***

Randy had gone exploring with his daddy the same summer they had moved to the mountain. Their hike in the woods had been enjoyable, but very vigorous, and when they
found the big wide spot in the river it was extremely inviting. There was a large washed out spot in the riverbank where there was hardly any current. The surface of the still water had been sparkling that day. The sun was shining down through the massive pine trees and made a beautiful reflection on the water. It only took one suggestion from Bob, and they had shucked their sweaty clothes and dived in. Both were excellent swimmers, even though Randy was only seven years old then. They were active in the YMCA near where they had lived in the city and swam frequently together.

8

Even with all their swimming experiences, they had never enjoyed a swim as much as they were that warm afternoon in July. For one thing, they had never been skinny-dipping, and swimming naked in the cool, clear water was wonderful. They felt like dolphins and swam around and around as if the pool was never ending.

Bob was playing one of their favorite games; diving under Randy, grabbing him by the legs and throwing him high into the air. They were laughing and Randy squealed with joy. On one of his launches into the forest air, he got a glimpse of someone moving around on the bank of the river. Before Randy could tell Bob, he had thrown him high into the air again. Randy tried to see who it was on the riverbank, but he wasn't turned the right way.

"Daddy, Daddy!" he gasped. He was having a hard time getting his father's attention, because Bob kept going back under the water.

"Daddy, look! Someone took our clothes!" he shouted, coughing and spitting, and gasping for air. When Bob heard those words, Randy had his full attention and as he treaded water, he looked at his son.

"What did you say?" he said, not quite sure he heard right.

Randy wiped the water from his face and pointed toward the shore, "Someone took our clothes, Daddy!"

Bob swam a little ways toward the shore, and called, "Who's out there? What are you doing there?"

He and Randy could see someone moving around in the trees, but it did not seem as if they were trying to leave. The grassy spot where they had dropped their clothes was empty, and Bob felt a little sick at the thought of going home stark naked!

Randy said in a whisper "Daddy, listen!"

They could hear the sound of children giggling, and Bob knew immediately it was some kids playing a prank. He was angry and relieved at the same time.

"You kids come on out here and put our clothes back! You just wait till your parents find out about this!" He tried to be stern, but his mind was flashing back to a similar day in his childhood. He and his buddies had done the same thing to a group of girls. He could remember what great fun it had been.

About that time, two small blonde-headed boys came out into the open. Now, Randy and Bob had their turn at giggling. The boys were wearing Bob's clothes. One had his blue jeans on, pulled up under his arms with Bob's cap perched backward on his head. The other boy had Bob's shirt on, hanging down to his knees and was wearing his size eleven boots. They were carrying Randy's clothes and came stumbling over to the riverbank. They looked really comical and were laughing so hard that they could hardly talk.

"You guys looking for these?" they said in unison. It wasn't until that moment that Bob realized that they were identical twins.

Susan always thought of Bob's story of that day whenever the swimming hole was mentioned. It was just a small part of that first glorious summer here on the mountain. In four short years, they had made so many memories and friends.

***

As she passed the sandwiches out to the boys, the telephone rang. She signaled the boys to have a little silent prayer of thanks as she reached to answer the insistent ring.

It was the twins' mother, Mary Martin. She was wondering if her boys had come over there already. They

10

had rushed off without breakfast and she was concerned. Susan assured her they were eating and told her that they all promised to bring fish home for lunch.

Susan watched the boys gobble up their food while she talked to Mary. They were nearly finished when she got off the telephone.

"Can we go now, Mama?" Randy was eager to be off and to try to catch that big fish which had eluded them for so long.

"Yes, Honey. Do you have some of that special bait you wanted to try? I hope you do better than last time!" She laughed, remembering how Kelley had fallen into the water after getting too excited, and how the fish had gotten away ... again! The boys had talked about that adventure for hours afterward.

"'That was your mother on the phone," she told the twins. "You be sure to bring her a big mess of fish, too!"

Susan went to the doorway and watched as the boys rushed off in the direction of the river. She leaned against the door and smiled, thinking what a fortunate woman she was.

***

As she stood there, June came around the corner of the house with a basket of berries. Her curly, dark hair framed her lovely, young face, which was flushed with excitement.

"Mom, can we make pie for lunch?" June was unusually bright and cheerful that morning, and was up earlier than normal. Susan was surprised to see her outside rather than spending hours in the bathroom in front of the mirror. She was a normal young teenager and this morning, her interest was domestic. She had

11

always had a strong interest in the home and cooking, doing more than most would expect.

"Sure, Babe," Susan put her arm around June and they went into the cabin. "But first, you can help me fix your Daddy's breakfast," she said with a smile.

The day had started out beautifully. None of them knew what horror and worry was ahead. None of them knew their lives would never be the same.

Chapter 2

About mid-morning, Old Jack Barnes rode up to the cabin on Bucky, his favorite horse. Bob was out in the vegetable garden picking summer squash and tomatoes. They always had a beautiful garden and produced many, many jars of food for the long winter months.

"Looks like that might be your last mess of squash, Bob. You gonna have some for lunch? Yum, and vine ripe tomatoes, too? Yep, don't mind if I do!" Old Jack was always a welcome visitor at the Greyson's home. He had become a good friend to them and could always cheer up the saddest, hurt little boy or disheartened young girl.

"You bet, Old Jack!" Bob looked up from his picking with a smile. "But you better watch out…Susan just might put you to washing dishes or sweeping floors," he teased.

Old Jack laughed heartily, and got down off his horse. He led him over to the creek, which flowed by only yards from the front doorway of the cabin. While the buckskin drank from the cold mountain water, Old Jack told of his ride that morning.

***

He had ridden through the woods behind the little town. Everyone referred to that area as "behind" because there was only one paved road going into Madison, and no main road going out the other side. It was nestled at the foot of rolling mountains, which towered above, seemingly forever.

The river ran down the mountain behind the town. It was of great use to the townspeople, because it supplied their electrical power and was of much importance to the transportation of huge trees from higher up in the hills. The saw mill was located on the banks of the river a few miles up from Madison. The logging roads leading up there were, in fact, the only roads on that side of town. The electrical plant was about a mile outside the city limits, providing many townspeople with jobs, as did the saw mill.

Old Jack had been out to the little cemetery where his wife, Rachel, was buried. His visits there were regular, yet they were not as painful as they had been in the past. His friendship with the Greysons had given him a new "family" and someone to love again. They had shared something precious with him that could never be replaced.

"Looked like someone had been out to Rachel's grave just this morning, Bob."

He had told Bob several times lately of finding fresh flowers on the grave, and he wasn't sure who was putting them there. He had an idea that it was June, because she had asked him to tell her all about Rachel only a few weeks before. She had asked many questions and the telling had brought tears to old Jack's eyes. June seemed truly touched and had cried openly, as old Jack held her awkwardly in his arms.

"I'm more and more convinced that it must be June, but I don't know if I should ask her or not. What do you think?" Old Jack was appreciative of June's attentions, but wasn't sure that she should dwell on it so much.

Bob leaned against a tree in front of the cabin, still holding the basket of squash on one arm. He gazed up into the trees and shook his head.

"Well, Old Jack...I don't know. If it is her, surely it doesn't do her any harm, reckon? She seems to be so

14

saddened by the fact that she never knew Rachel...we all are. I'll talk to June if you want me to, but I really think it will pass." He put a hand on Old Jack's shoulder, feeling very close to the man.

"Dad? Old Jack?" June stepped out of the cabin, rubbing a dishtowel between her hands. Having heard their last words, she asked in puzzlement, "Are you talking about me?"

Bob's black eyebrows arched upward, as the two men looked at each other. Old Jack said, "Yeah, we were, Sugar. I was over to Rachel's grave this morning and saw fresh flowers there. We figured it might be you doing it." He raised his bushy eyebrows as he looked intently at the young girl.

"Oh, yes, Old Jack! I did take some flowers over there a coupla times, but not lately. I found fresh flowers already there both times I went, so I put mine on a grave that didn't have any. Why?"

Old Jack scratched his head, "Now that's odd. There were fresh flowers today and have been so much all along. If you didn't do it, then I wonder who did."

"Not much telling. You two had a lot of friends, didn't you?" June shaded her eyes as she looked down the path. "You guys haven't seen Randy, have you? He was supposed to bring some fish back for lunch. If we're going to have a fish fry, we have to get 'em cleaned and cut in time to cook 'em up!" Playfully, she put her fisted hands on her hips.

June liked to have lunch on the table right at twelve o'clock. In fact, she was more particular about it than her mother. During the summer, she had done a lot of the cooking and had even started preparing many meals without the help of her mother. It was good practice, and besides, she loved doing it. Some of her

15

friends could not imagine what kind of fun she could get out of being in a hot kitchen so much.

"No, I haven't seen him since early this morning, but he should be back by now." He turned at the sound of someone whistling, and saw the boy walking up the road. "And there he is! I knew he would be right on time." Bob smiled and winked at Old Jack.

June laughed, "He looks like Tom Sawyer! Don't you think so, Daddy?" The boy did make a picture for sure. He walked barefoot, with his pants legs rolled up. His sneakers were tied together, socks stuffed inside, and draped around his neck. He had his fishing pole over one shoulder and had a nice string of fish in the other hand.

"Now all you need is a bandage on your big toe!" June laughed. She took the fish and bustled away, then turning back with a mock sternness she rebuked Randy. "It's about time you got here!"

"What's the matter with her?" Randy asked as he put down his gear.

"Well, what makes you ask a question like that? She's a girl isn't she…Tom Sawyer?" quipped Old Jack.

Randy grinned and looked down at his bare feet. Wiggling his toes, he laughed, "I guess all I need *is* a bandage on my big toe!"

"Well, Son, tell me about the fishing. Did the other boys catch as many as you did?" Bob enjoyed fishing as much as Randy. They went often and put lots of fish in their freezer for winter. They even smoked some and then Susan would can it. The tasty meat was a rare treat on a cold winter day.

"We had a blast, Dad! But Kenny and Kelly together didn't catch as many as I did all by myself! When I left, they said they were going down the river to another place they wanted to try. I think they are gonna try the other side, past Watson's bridge. We didn't catch that old big fish, though, and Kenny said the monster was giving them bad luck." He put his hands on his hips and laughed. "Can you believe that? Ha!" He enjoyed the rivalry that they all three shared when fishing, hunting, swimming, or anything. Always one trying to out-do the other.

"Well, you come with me fishing one of these days, and I'll show you how to fish!" Old Jack always had to get in on the competition, and never failed to have a teasing word for the boy.

Later, with June smiling sweetly, they sat down to a delicious meal of fried fish and country fried potatoes. It was exactly twelve o'clock. Bob's morning mess of squash had been prepared and with June's berry pie, the meal was delicious.

***

The atmosphere and companionship had been most pleasant, so the men were quite satisfied as they moved into the living area and propped their weary feet up, relaxing comfortably. Randy had followed them and sat with his feet up and chewing on a toothpick. He was very drowsy and sat with his eyes half closed. He was unaware of the grown-up conversation, but the rumble of the men's deep voices talking quietly was soothing and comfortable.

Randy looked absently toward the fireplace, and thought how funny it looked with plants on the hearth and no fire. Why put plants on a fireplace, he wondered. It didn't make much sense to him.

He jumped when the telephone rang. "I'll get it!" His mother and sister were busy doing dishes.

He was not surprised that it was Mary Martin, because she and his mother talked frequently. But he was surprised at the reason she had called.

17

When he got off the phone, he turned with a puzzled look on his face. "Daddy, the twins haven't come home yet," he said.

"What did Mary say?" Susan asked him.

"She just wondered if they were here, and had we left the river together. She sure sounded worried." He rubbed his forehead, and then shrugged. "Oh well, she said she will call back when they come in...I bet they're really gonna get it!"

"Do you think you ought to go down to the river and see if you can find them?" Susan asked Bob. She knew that if it were Randy who was this late, she would want someone to go and see about him.

Bob agreed. "Randy and I can saddle up the mares and go down that way. Jack, would you like to go along with us? It's a nice day to take a ride anyway," Bob said, as he shoved his cap onto his head.

"Sure thing, and Bucky's all set.! I bet we'll find those young-uns out there on a hot streak. When I get one of those, I can hardly drag myself away," he laughed, rubbing his full stomach.

***

They went out, and within a few minutes were on their way down the road toward the creek trail. They could see Randy's barefoot tracks on the moist dirt where he had returned that morning.

"Boy, are they gonna catch it when they get home!" Randy repeated. He knew that Kenny and Kelly's parents felt the same as his did about being on time. The three boys even helped each other to remember when it was time to head home.

"Yeah, I know," replied his father, "that's why I don't understand their being late. It is pretty unusual for

18

them." Bob had always admired the obedience of the two boys.

After their horses crossed the clear, cold water of the creek, they took another trail. It ran from the creek to where the boys usually met the river when they went to their favorite fishing hole. It was not as well beaten as the other one had been. Usually, Bob's family or friends were the only ones to use it.

As they met the trail which ran beside the river, they heard another horse coming. That was not unusual for this area, because nearly everyone had a horse of one kind or another.

It was Larry Miller, the young man who was working at the Martin's grocery store. When he heard that the twins had not come in, and saw how upset Mrs. Martin was, he had volunteered to go look for them.

"Hello, there," he shouted. He was a quiet likeable young man, only nineteen. He had graduated from the high school just over a year ago, and had gone to work at Tom Martin's store. He said he did not want to go to college, because he had no desire to leave Madison. Most everyone knew the main reason he loved it so much was because of his best girl, Jill Clark. She was eighteen and had graduated the previous spring. They had plans to be married at Christmas time.

"Are you looking for the twins, too?" Larry said when he caught up with them.

"Yes, thought we'd remind them what time it is so they can git on home and git in trouble!" Bob laughed, trying to cover the concern of his heavy heart. "What are you doing out here? Don't you work on Saturdays?"

"Yes, I do, but Tom let me come look for the boys, so Mrs. Martin wouldn't be so worried. Do you know where they went fishing?"

Randy spoke up, feeling important. "I do! We went together to our favorite fishing hole. I caught all I needed and went home," he said proudly. "They were goin' on down the river to another spot. Kenny said that monster fish we can't catch was givin' them bad luck! Ha!"

"We might as well ride together," Old Jack commented. "Four sets of eyes are better than three, I always say!"

"Aww, I bet you never said that in your life," Randy laughed, as the old man reached over and tousled his hair. Love swelled in his heart for the boy.

***

The boy just did not know how serious this could be, Bob thought. Well, it won't turn out that way, he told himself positively. After all, there are lots of things to attract eleven-year-old boys out here in these woods, he assured himself, as he sat straighter in the saddle and squared his shoulders.

Before long, they had come to the boys' favorite fishing and swimming hole. Randy pointed and spoke up with a deep, official-sounding voice.

"This is where we separated. You can see my tracks where I took off my shoes, right before I started home."

Randy was enjoying playing detective, and got down off the mare and began looking for their tracks, too.

"Didn't you say they were going down river, Son? Across Watson's bridge?" Bob asked, relishing his son's antics.

"Yessir. Oh, here are their tracks going into the woods. But they stop when they get to the pine needles here."

The young boy walked all bent over studying the ground. Then he stood up and said importantly, "I guess we might as well just ride on down river and then we'll find them."

Old Jack winked at Bob…both men knew already that they would do just that. Bob grinned, "Well, come on, Sherlock, let's go then!"

Randy gave a big grin to his father as he hurried over and mounted his horse, urging her on as the others followed.

***

The group found no other trace of the twins as far as they went. They called and called, but no one answered. They crossed the river at Watson's bridge and went a good distance with no results at all. Things were very bleak and around five o'clock, they decided to turn back.

"Maybe they already got home. After all, they could have gone another way," Larry tried to reassure the group. He had grown up with a responsible attitude because his father had died when he was a small boy. He had been a strong person for his mother, Faye, all his growing years. He had helped her and his two younger sisters, Linda and Brenda, have a stable, happy life. His mother was kept busy as organist in the church and her family was sincerely dedicated to serving God. Larry hoped his mother would remarry someday. He had seen the sadness in her face many times, and he knew that it was loneliness.

The group reluctantly turned their horses and headed for home. As they separated where the trails divided, Bob turned to Larry. "Will you be sure to call us if the boys are there? I bet they are! In fact, they've probably already had their whippin'," the older man said with a wry smile.

   "Yep, I'll call when I get there…and I bet they're home, too. I'm gonna tell those little rascals I got saddle sores because of them!" They all laughed as Larry galloped away.

Chapter 3

The sun was setting earlier every evening, now that summer was virtually over. The stars were already shining when Randy, Bob, and Old Jack rode up to the cabin. Susan had heard the horses approaching and had gone out to meet the group.

"Did you find them? We've been worried sick! Mary just called a little while ago and said they haven't come in yet!" Her voice and her face betrayed how anxious she was.

Bob looked at Old Jack, who shook his head wearily. Then he turned to Susan as he got off his horse. "No, Honey, we didn't find them. I don't know where they could be," Bob said as he tied the animal.

Susan's face was pale, and she did not say anything, as she pressed a closed fist against her mouth. Bob did not like her reaction, and put his arms around her, knowing how she felt. Anytime a child had any kind of problem, she felt the pain as if it were her own child.

"Maybe they went off with someone from the country and forgot to call in," he said unconvincingly.

June had come out onto the porch and stood quietly, leaning against the door frame.

"Daddy, you all must be hungry. Don't you want to come in and eat some supper?" She felt she had to do something to break the awful tension that hung in the air.

Old Jack knew what she was thinking, and said, "Sure, Darlin'! We're starvin'! Come on fellas, let's eat!"

They all went on into the house and Susan and June fixed everyone a plate of food. They sat around the table and joined hands for prayer.

Bob prayed "Heavenly Father, we thank You for the food before us and ask You to bless it. We praise

You for Your presence in all our lives. Father, we ask You to watch over Kenny and Kelly and keep them safe wherever they are, and Lord, please help Tom and Mary have peace. We thank You for Your Son that You gave for our salvation, and that You are always with us. In Jesus' name we pray, Amen."

As the group ate their food in silence, each struggled with his own grim thoughts. The sudden ring of the telephone startled everyone and they simultaneously jumped to answer it.

Susan was nearest, and answered with an expectant, "Hello?"

The group waited in silence, leaning forward motionless as she talked. They knew immediately that there was no news.

"Bob, maybe you ought to talk to Tom," Susan said, handing him the receiver. She shook her head to the group as she slowly sat down. Quietly they listened to Bob's end of the conversation, trying to figure out what the plans were.

Several men had agreed to form a search party, but that would have to wait till morning light. Everyone in the country had been telephoned and no one had seen the twins. The community was pulling together, and they all agreed to keep their outside lights on all night as a guide for the boys if they were lost in the woods. The few who did not have telephones were notified by neighbors what to do. Anyone seeing the boys was to keep them in one place and call the grocery store immediately. It was to be the headquarters for the search.

No one slept much that night, praying and wondering what could have happened to the boys. They were never apart and it was certain that where they found one they would find the other. Their family and friends worried about those small boys being alone all night in the woods.

***

It had been two weeks and fourteen long, sleepless nights. Still the boys had not been found. Everyone who possibly could do so joined a search party and had combed the wooded hills. Around-the-clock-prayer-groups had been assigned to seek guidance and help from the Lord.

Search parties went up and down the river on either side but all they found were the two fishing poles. It was Jerry Davis who actually found them. Jerry was a red-haired, bearded young man. He was much shorter than most of his friends and heavier as well. He had a red face with blue eyes squinting out from his puffy cheeks. He was a quiet fellow, with an apparent gruffness that covered his tender attitude toward life.

The poles had been found in such an obvious place that Bob and the others could not understand how they had missed them before, and Jerry nearly did not see them at all. They were lying next to the river on the grassy bank. It even looked like a good spot for fishing. Jerry thought the boys might have been fishing there, but he was concerned that there was a very rocky, swift current only yards from the bank. Here the deep pool was calm and almost clear. It was small and shaded and a perfect place for fish to hide away from the swift currents of the river. But those same swift currents could easily sweep away two small boys if they had fallen in. His stomach churned with dread and it brought a lump to Jerry's throat to think of such a thing.

***

Mary Martin had been hysterical when Jerry told her. She, along with everyone else, felt sure that her boys had somehow fallen into the river. After the initial shock, Mary began to show an inner strength that even Susan could not understand. Then Mary tried to reassure Susan, and said she knew all things worked together for good for those who love the Lord.

Susan had not been able to let her own children out of sight since the twins had disappeared. She had her own secret thought that they had come to some kind of foul play, and had the hideous feeling that somehow the other children could be in danger.

Every time she closed her eyes she remembered holding Mary close that awful day, and the horrible deep sobbing that wracked both their bodies. Mary's pain had been so intense, so grief stricken that Susan shuddered to remember. Even Mary's words of reassurance since then could not erase the dreadful memory of Mary's pain.

Why, God? Why, she thought as she lay in bed at night. Why? They were just babies. Babies! And their parents love You so much. Why would You let a thing like this happen? She was very angry with God, and for the first time since that first glorious summer, her world seemed to be flipping over and over.

After the twins had met Bob and Randy at the swimming hole, the two families had become fast friends. It was not long before Bob and Susan knew the Martins had something very special in their lives. Soon, they began to have long talks about the Lord Jesus Christ and how His presence in a person's life could give them peace…peace that passes all understanding. Susan could remember Tom's and Mary's radiant faces as they shared the Good News of the Bible with her and Bob. Then there had been that wondrous day when on their knees they had accepted Christ as their Savior and knew that they could rest in Him always. In Him was the peace and tranquility they had longed for.

But, Susan had no peace. She had never felt farther from God than she did now, hurting, confused and scared.

***

It had been a long two weeks, and in the early morning light, Bob chopped firewood that he had neglected to chop for days. With each swing of his powerful arms, he became more and more tense at the realization they might never find the boys. Small search parties still went out in shifts, though hopes of finding them dwindled with each passing day. While Bob worked, he was unaware that a group of searchers were only minutes away from finding the bodies.

Jack and three other men had camped in the woods overnight, planning to return to town in the morning. They were cleaning up camp, and as Old Jack poured the remains of their coffee on the fire, one of the men suggested that they ride back to town along the river banks. They had searched every inch of that area of woods, and had been up and down the river. It would be easier traveling home that way. They could look there one more time.

The men agreed, and when they started out, two of them crossed the river there where it was fairly shallow and they rode abreast, two on each side of the river. The river had been a raging torrent for days after the rainstorm that came a few days after the boys' disappearance. Today, at last, it was flowing normally.

***

It was Old Jack who saw them first. He was riding along, thinking how hopeless the whole thing was.

27

He heard a rustling in the trees, and turned, seeing several animals scampering off in the opposite direction. He reined his horse, and went to take a look. This was a washout which led down to the bend in the riverbank and there were low bushes that met over the gully.

Old Jack got down off the buckskin horse and forced his way into the thick brush. The stench was awful. As he pushed a branch from his face, the sight before him almost made him wish he had never gotten off the horse.

There were two small bodies lying not far from one another. They were severely decayed, and had been damaged by wild animals. There were tracks of several kinds of animals all around and evidence of their attempts to tear through the clothing and eat the flesh. There was no doubt that it was the Martin twins. Jack could tell by their size and identical red flannel shirts.

"Dear merciful Jesus…" he quietly whispered. For a moment, all he could do was stand while the tears poured down his ruddy face.

"Over here! I found them!" Old Jack could barely choke out the words. He could visualize the reaction of the twins' family, and he was sickened by his thoughts.

Horror was the mutual reaction of the men who made their way across the river and through the thicket into the little clearing. It was evident that the bodies had washed up into the little place while the river was running high and ferociously after that storm.

Jerry Davis was with them that morning, and was aghast. "What do you think happened to them? I can't believe this…how are we ever going to tell their parents?" He stood almost frozen in place, asking aloud all the things each man was thinking. His red face showed concern as he uneasily began shifting from one foot to the other, his short legs pumping up and down.

"I don't know. All I do know is that we need to get the sheriff and take these boys to town," Old Jack replied. He walked to his horse and got his sleeping bag. Unrolling it, he numbly went toward the bodies feeling sick in the pit of his stomach. He unzipped the bag, and took the quilt out, and carefully laid the bag over one body. Then he gently laid the blue and white quilt over the other. Suddenly, Jerry rushed away and vomited violently.

"You two stay here with the bodies, and Jerry and I will go get the sheriff and tell their parents. It won't be long until someone will be back. Is that alright with both of you?" Handing Jerry his large red handkerchief, he took a deep breath and shook his head. He knew it would be unpleasant to stay but also knew that no one wanted to have to tell Tom and Mary Martin the tragic news.

They were about six miles downriver from Madison, and Old Jack knew it would take quite some time to go all the way into town. So, he headed for the nearest neighbor with a telephone which was Bob and Susan Greyson.

*⁎⁎

Bob had finished splitting wood and had it stacked beside the house. Then he'd carried part of it inside and had filled the boxes beside each of the fireplaces and the wood cookstove.

Susan had finished breakfast dishes, and had taken her treasured potted plants from the hearth of the fireplace. Then Bob had built a fire, which would become a regular chore each morning as the days grew cooler. Heat from the wood cook stove was welcomed in the earlier hours of morning.

They sat together drinking coffee, mesmerized by the jumping flames. Their somber mood kept them from enjoying the fire as they usually did. June and Randy were in the room, too, watching Saturday morning television shows.

"I can't believe it has been two whole weeks since the twins disappeared," Susan said quietly to Bob. She sat leaning forward, elbows on her knees with her mug cradled in both hands.

"Me either, Baby...and I'm beginning to wonder if we are ever going to find them." Bob felt grim about the situation along with the entire community. There had been numerous comments about the futility of the search.

Susan glanced at Bob and hesitated, not really wanting to say what she felt must be said. "Bob...do you think something got them? I just can't seem to get that idea out of my head." Susan's feelings about the disappearance had never been said aloud until now. She had been so frightened and angry. The fear was keeping her awake at night, and she had dark circles under her eyes. She knew she had to talk about it soon. It was becoming too much for her to bear.

As Bob looked into her tear-filled eyes, he could see the anguish and fear there. He gently put an arm around her and opened his mouth to say the reassuring words she needed.

Before he could speak, they heard the sounds of horses approaching. They glanced at one another, then rose at the same time and went outside quietly, without disturbing the children.

They stood on the front steps watching the two riders come into the yard. Susan reached for Bob's hand when she saw the expression on Old Jack's face.

"Jack?" It was all she could muster. There was a cold feeling in her heart and she had a growing lump in her throat. Her hands moved to either side of her face.

Jack nodded his head as he got down off his horse. "We found 'em," he said somberly. His insides were feeling terribly sick.

"Are they…?" Susan was shaking with dread. She clutched Bob's arm, waiting to hear the words they all feared. Bob's arm went firmly around her shoulders.

"Where are they?" Bob knew by the men's faces that the boys must be dead.

"We found them about three miles from here," Jerry said softly. He thought if this was any example of how hard it would be to tell the twins' parents, he sure didn't want to tell them. He still felt the gruesome nausea in his stomach.

"That close? Why on earth didn't we find them sooner?" Bob could not believe that they had been so close all along.

Susan sobbed as she turned and rushed inside the cabin. This was the moment they had all waited for, yet she was not prepared for the hardness of the actual truth.

"Well, Bob, they were up in a sort of gully with brush all around. The river evidently washed them up there during that storm last week. I wouldn't have found them if it hadn't been for a bunch of animals that were…well…" Old Jack could not form the words, again feeling that sickness in the pit of his own stomach.

Bob sensed his feelings and said, "What a dreadful day, Jack. Why don't the two of you come on in? I'll fix you a cup of coffee, and then I'll go on into town with you."

He had stepped down off the porch and put his arm across Old Jack's shoulders. He urged him up the steps and into the cabin. Jerry followed, head lowered and dreading the rest of the events of the day. He stopped on the porch and took off his hat. Vigorously he rubbed his bearded face and the back of his red neck with his chubby hands.

When they went in the door, they heard quiet sobbing. The old western movie had been turned off, and Susan sat with her two children in her arms. They all cried openly and with agonizing grief. Susan felt guilty because she was so relieved that it had not been her own children. Randy was thinking how he would never, never see his two friends again, while June was horrified and could not understand why someone so young had to die.

They all looked up when the men came into the room. Susan sobbed, "How are we ever going to tell Tom and Mary?"

Bob went over to her and as she stood, he put his arms around her. He could feel the tears coming to his own eyes, and blinked them back, trying to be strong for his family. That was useless, as the tears flowed down and dripped into Susan's dark hair.

"Oh, Daddy!" June went to her father for comfort, and Randy followed. He cried, "Is it really true? I didn't want them to die!" His sobs were too much for his father, and as Bob put his arms around his family, he too shared their tears, his making hot tracks down his face.

Jerry, standing in the doorway, turned on his heel and quietly slipped outside. Weeping, he stumbled over to a tall pine by the creek.

***

Old Jack went into the bedroom where he knew there was a telephone. He felt he had to get out of that room before he exploded. He was very angry that something so tragic could have happened in their little town. Things had been quiet and peaceful for so many years. Even when someone had passed on, it had been from illness or old age. There had only been one fatal accident at the saw mill in all the years he could remember.

What was his name? Oh, yeah, Henry Dumas. Henry had moved into the area to get away from a police charge. He had been killed instantly when he carelessly knocked a lever loose which held a huge thick log above where he stood.

When the police traced his family to notify them of his death, they found he was wanted on a burglary charge. No one in Madison had any connection with him. Everyone was very detached but felt sad that an accident had happened. Poor old Henry, Old Jack thought as he remembered.

Sitting wearily on the side of the bed, he slowly dialed the sheriff's office and asked for Sheriff Billings. He quietly told the officer about their discovering the bodies of the young boys. Sheriff Billings asked about the exact location and wanted to know who was still there.

He said he would send an ambulance as close as they could get to the location, then they would go on in by horseback and carry the bodies out that way. He wanted to know if he should notify the parents or if someone else would be telling them.

"Well, I had more or less planned on telling them since I was the one who actually found them. But it might be better if you do send someone over from your office. I don't know if I could face those folks with this kind of news."

Old Jack had always considered himself a strong person, but this would be the hardest thing he would ever try to do, and he decided that he just couldn't do it at all.

The sheriff agreed to go over himself and tell the family. He said he would do it after they brought the bodies in. He was afraid they might want to go to the location and he knew that would be too hard on them.

After Old Jack hung up the phone, he sat with his elbows on his knees staring out the window where he could see poor Jerry by the big pine. This was such a hard thing... why, Lord? Why? Jesus, help us all here. We really need you now.

***

Later that next week there was a funeral held for the boys. Everyone from town was there, and all the businesses closed for the afternoon. Pastor Jordan wept openly as he offered condolences and reassurance for the family.

"Kenny and Kelly were sunshine in all our lives and I thank God that He lent them to us for a while. We can take comfort knowing they are home in the arms of Jesus and that those of us who know Him as our Savior will again see Kenny and Kelly's smiling faces."

The church choir sang for the services, ending with "Jesus Loves the Little Children". It was a devastating experience for the members of the community. Nearly everyone had been to one funeral or another, but no one was prepared for the sight of the two small caskets at the front of the chapel.

Tom and Mary had already resigned themselves to the probability that their boys might be dead, and after the painful news had come, they had held up rather well. Their daughter, Wilma, had taken it the hardest of the family, weeping brokenheartedly during the entire service. Her parents knew that she was all they had now, and with God's help, they would be strong for her.

34

After the long days and nights of waiting, the funeral had almost seemed like a whole separate tragedy in itself. Tom and Mary were on either side of Wilma as they left the chapel that cool, early fall day. The memory of that sight stayed with the townspeople for a long time to come. The twins were buried side by side in the little cemetery outside of town, across the river.

It seemed ironic that they would be buried beside the same river that most of the people felt had taken the lives of the two little boys. They had loved the river though and it also seemed perfectly appropriate. No one could know that this was only the beginning.

Chapter 4

Bob did not understand what had happened to their world. He just knew that it had not been the same. Susan would not take her walks anymore and he never heard her sing. She still had the feeling that someone or something had taken the twins that awful day. She simply would not accept the obvious fact that they had drowned. He had tried desperately to soothe her anger toward God, and had prayed so often for the Lord to strengthen her.

Bob had not told Susan yet, but in Drayton, not far away, someone had disappeared about the same time the twins had. The man had never been found, and the people had only recently given up the search. They had lost all hopes of finding him. The river was much rougher near that area, and they felt he had been forever lost in the swift currents. Bob knew that Susan would be sure to hear about it sooner or later, and he knew it would not help her mood.

***

It had been several weeks since the boys' funeral and most people were trying to carry on with their lives. There was still a hint of uneasiness among some of the parents in their village. Any time a child dies under strange circumstances, parents are wary and more than a little concerned.

There was a slight breeze that morning in early October. The air was brisk and the leaves were turning colors. Bob was wishing Susan would be more interested in the forest again, as he checked the oil in his old blue pickup. It seems like she is afraid now, he thought, and that's just no good. If only it could be like before. He was getting ready to go into town for some supplies and as usual, he felt uneasy about going.

He had tried to convince her that one of the twins had probably fallen into the river and the other tried to save him. The current must have been too strong and they were beaten against the rocks and washed down river. But she continued to believe that something or even someone had gotten them, and she refused to let the kids out of her sight when they were not in school. She would not even leave the place without Bob or a neighbor.

On the days he was not working at the saw mill, he tried to stay close to home and reassure Susan by being relaxed and natural.

"Susan, I'm going into town to get some parts for the pressure pump. Do you need anything, or do you want to go?" He asked hopefully. The pump on their well had been squeaking and the pressure had been uneven lately. He knew he had better fix it or they might be without running water.

Susan paled, and thought that she couldn't bear for him to leave today. But she knew how worried he had been about her, and so she decided to try and cheer up if only so that he would not fret.

"No, Honey, I guess I'll stay today. You can bring some sugar and a jug of milk from Pete's Dairy, if you will," she spoke much too quickly, and was unaware that she did so.

Bob noticed her nervousness, but tried not to let her know. He said reassuringly, "I won't be gone long. I can take Randy if he wants to go, unless you'd rather he stay."

"Do you care if he stays?" She felt like his presence would be a comfort, and she did not want him to leave, too.

"Randy, you stay here and keep your mother company, okay?" Bob knew that Randy had missed going into town alone with him, but he also knew that Susan needed the boy for a distraction.

"Sure, Daddy," Randy replied cheerfully. He had some plans of his own for the morning, and had hopes of making things right in their world again.

As he turned and went into the house, Randy patted his Mother on the arm. Susan's mouth fell open, and she nearly laughed, thinking how mature her eleven year old was trying to act. Immediately, she thought how selfish she had been lately, and how she seemed to have no control over her fears. She took a deep breath, and went into the garden and began pulling up the dried plants. She knew if she kept busy, she could keep from thinking.

There was a Scripture going around and around in her head, though, as she knelt. Isaiah 41:10…I must go look that up when I'm done here, she thought.

Bob had noticed Randy patting his mother's arm and smiled.

"Okay, then, I will see you later," he said. Knowing Susan, he added, "I won't be gone long, Dear, and I will be careful."

***

The old blue pickup started instantly. It always did have the best hum to it and never gave him any trouble. His favorite past time was to work on it and keep it running perfectly.

As he pulled away from the cabin, he turned and waved to Susan who was kneeling in the garden with a bunch of dry plants in one hand. She waved the other and yelled goodbye as cheerfully as she could muster.

He gave her a big smile as he drove off, and began to pray. "Lord, comfort her and give her strength.

38

She is Your child and I put her in Your hands. In the Name of Jesus I pray."

Somehow, Bob felt better then, and as he drove away, he thought what a beautiful morning it was. The leaves trembled in the chilly fall air. He always enjoyed driving into their little village along this road. It was very beautiful with many lush trees, soft green grasses, and very often wild animals darted across the road or sat quietly watching as he passed by.

This time of the year was his favorite as there were colorful fall flowers everywhere, and the deep red of the turning maple leaves was striking. He watched for squirrels as he rode along. He and Randy had a game they played when they went to town together. They would see how many squirrels they could count between their cabin and town. Occasionally, they would see as many as a dozen, especially this time of year when they gathered nuts for the long winter months.

There was a bend in the road a little ways before it came to the one lane wooden bridge which went over the river. As Bob turned the old truck to go around the bend, it sputtered and died.

"Now what in the world?" Bob said aloud. He could not imagine what was wrong with his faithful old truck.

He slapped his hands down on the steering wheel in irritation. This was just what he needed to make his trip to town longer! "Lord, give me strength," he thought.

He got out and went around to the front of the pickup. It was one of the rare times that he felt anger toward the thing. He jerked up the hood and checked the engine. From all indications, he was simply out of gas.

"Out of gas? Now how could that be…?" Bob knew the gauge showed at least a half a tank. The dumb thing was busted! Bob thought with dread, what bad timing this was.

He left the hood raised, and as he briskly started walking he promised himself that he would never be without a five-gallon can of gas again! The bad thing was he knew that there were two at the cabin in the well house. They were stored along with sleeping bags, extra blankets, lanterns, a shovel, and other safety equipment that they always carried along in the winter, regardless of the weather.

"But that doesn't do me a bit of good right now!" he said aloud as he walked.

At the sound of his voice, the bushes beside the road parted suddenly with a racket. Bob jumped, and his heart hammered in his chest. He could not remember when he had been so startled. He was relieved to see that it was just their dog, Husky.

"Susan's mood must be rubbing off on me," he said to the dog as he stooped to pat him on the head. "Did you decide to take a shortcut and go with me into the village, old fella?"

Bob surprised himself at the use of the word "village". He had never quite gotten used to using that word, even though all the local people did. Where he had grown up, he had rarely even heard the word.

As they walked, Bob watched Husky's muscles ripple under his shiny black coat. They had had him since he was a newborn puppy, long before they came here. He had been like a member of the family for many years, and had been happier here in the open than ever before. Bob wished that Husky had stayed home with Susan this morning, though. He knew that the large dog gave Susan a little more confidence when he was around.

After a little while, Bob began to relax and enjoy the walk. He was beginning to see what Susan had loved about her walks. He felt sad knowing that she had quit taking them. It was so quiet except for forest sounds and here on the bridge the sounds of the river were so very refreshing. As they crossed the one lane bridge, Bob was entranced by the movements of the water below. He stopped for a minute to gaze into its icy depths.

Talking to God frequently was quite normal for Bob, and he found himself automatically in prayer as he stood there. "Dear Lord," he prayed under his breath, "Please help Susan…Your Word says in John 14:18 that You will not leave her comfortless and that You will come to her. Please, dear Lord, come to her soon! She needs You so much!"

"In Jesus' Name," he said aloud. As he watched the water rippling over the rocks below, he thought how ironic it was that something so beautiful could be so treacherous as to take the lives of the little Martin boys.

That thought made him realize that he had better be on his way. As he started to step off the wooden bridge, he noticed that Husky had suddenly rushed ahead of him.

"Husky! Come on back here! Stay on the road!" he shouted. But the dog did not want to come back. Something by the river had his attention. Such a ruckus! What on earth is that dog barking at, Bob wondered.

He hurried to where Husky had gone, and as he stepped into the clearing he was sickened by what he saw.

"Oh Lord!" he gasped, stopping short. He had trouble believing what was before his eyes. He had never seen a more gruesome sight in all his life! There blood everywhere, and the shredded part of what appeared to be a dead goat. It had not been eaten, but crazily, it was strewn all over the river bank. There were bear tracks all around and Husky was really acting funny. Bob walked around the clearing, thinking that the bear must have been very angry to do such a vicious thing. It occurred to him that perhaps the animal was ill or wounded. It was very odd that the goat had not been eaten, because the bears in the area usually only killed for food. Bob had never even heard of anyone near Madison being attacked by bears.

It's really weird, he thought, and I'm not about to just hang around here until it comes back. As he started back toward the road, he noticed some smaller bear tracks. Well, that must be it! Bob figured that it must have been a mama bear protecting her young ones. He felt some relief at the thought, because he sure didn't like the idea of a crazed bear wandering around their valley.

"Come on, Husky. Let's go on into town and get some gas," he said as he backed away. He thought he heard an unusual sound and turned around to see. The man was standing so close that Bob nearly bumped into him. Bob was not a small man himself, but he had to look up to see the face of the stranger. He was a giant of a man, Bob thought.

He was way over six feet tall and had very broad shoulders. His pants were ragged and torn and he had no shirt or shoes. His hair was as black as his big, bushy beard. It was sleek and shiny, almost out of place on the big man. His hands were covered with blood and he held them out to Bob, though he said nothing. There were tears in his eyes and he seemed to be trying to communicate with Bob. Bob caught his breath and reached toward the big man, thinking he was hurt. Suddenly, the stranger lunged into the brush and was gone. Husky did not follow, but stayed by Bob's side whining softly.

Bob stood there for several long minutes watching the place where the mysterious man had disappeared. Finally, he stooped down and scratched

Husky on his ears. It was obvious he and his dog were extremely puzzled by what they had seen.

As they walked the rest of the way into the village, Bob decided he would not mention seeing the big man or the dead goat. That and the bears would be enough to put Susan into a tailspin, he thought. He could not know how much he would regret that decision.

Soon, he came to the one and only gasoline stop in Madison. The Martin Grocery Store had two pumps in front that served the people in the area.

Bob went inside and explained how he had run out of gas and asked if Tom would let Larry drive him out to get his pickup. Of course, Tom was glad to help.

Before they left, though, Bob called Susan on the telephone to let her know he would be later than he had planned.

He was embarrassed to have run out of gas, and made a joke of it hoping to cheer Susan up. She seemed to react with humor, even teasing him as usual. Bob was delighted to hear a smile in her voice.

"I'll probably get a sandwich in town and will be in late this evening. I'm going to see about fixing that old gas gauge. Will you have a good hot supper ready for me?"

Susan replied, "Of course, Honey, and try not to run out of gas or have a flat on the way home, okay?"

Bob felt tremendous relief inside as he realized she sounded more natural and lighthearted than she had in weeks.

"I won't, and you can be sure I'm gonna keep one of those five gallon cans of gas in the pickup from now on!" he laughed.

"You'd better, Honey! Before you go I have to share something wonderful with you!"

Bob grinned at Tom Martin who was standing nearby. "Something wonderful? What?"

"Well, while I was in the garden after you left, a Bible verse kept going through my head…Isaiah 41:10…over and over. It was so strange. Well, I went in after a bit and looked it up because I couldn't remember what it said."

"And? What did Isaiah 41:10 say?" Bob said smiling triumphantly at Tom, knowing full well his prayers had been answered.

"Here, I'll read it to you," the happy voice answered. "Fear thou not; for I am with thee: I will uphold thee with the right hand of my righteousness," she read, choking back tears of relief. "Oh, Bob, it's all okay! It's okay!"

"I knew it would be, Dear. I can't wait till I get home and we can talk," he said tenderly with earnest gratitude in his voice. "God is good, isn't He?" Bob added softly. He glanced at Tom, who was smiling broadly.

"Oh, yes, Honey! Well, I'll let you go. I've got a lot of work to do! Oh, by the way, do you have Husky with you? We missed him this morning, but June thought she saw him following when you left. Did he?"

"Yep, the old fella is with me, Sugar. Keeps me company so's I don't miss you so much," Bob teased her lovingly.

***

That evening when Bob drove into the yard, he did not see anyone around. The lights were off inside the house, and he felt very strange. With a sense of apprehension, he turned off the ignition and lights. He sat in the darkness for a moment, trying to see if he could make out anything in the shadows. There were no movements of any kind and the night was filled with an eerie silence.

Quietly, Bob opened the pickup door. The echoing squeak made him jump. Cringing at the noise it made, he slowly and carefully got out. He gently shut the door, pulling it against the hinges to keep it from making another noise. Bob moved noiselessly around toward the front of the pickup, alert to any sound. The silence was terrifying…not even the dog was around to greet him.

Husky had left town earlier in the day and Bob had laughed, making a comment that Husky had to "get home to mama"! He remembered being relieved because he knew Susan would want the dog there.

Now, for some unknown reason, the dog was nowhere to be seen. And the family…where are they? Suddenly cold fear gripped Bob's heart. It's hammering seemed to break the stony silence. Bob held his breath, trying to silence the pumping of his own blood. He thought he heard a muffled gasp inside the cabin.

"Susan, where are you!?" he shouted. He grabbed the axe off the wooden porch as he rushed into the cabin. He was horrified to think what he might find.

"SURPRISE! SURPRISE!!" Instantly the lights flashed on and in a split second his whole family was engulfing him with hugs and kisses.

"Happy birthday, Daddy!" Bob could see through his misty eyes the pride on the face of his young son. He gazed around at his family delightedly bewildered.

"You forgot, didn't you, Daddy? Well, we didn't! Are you surprised? Are you?" Randy grabbed his father's hand and held it between his own and jumped up and down. It was impossible to contain his excitement.

"Hey, what is all this? A party?" Bob was so very glad to see his family excited and cheerful. They were fine and he felt foolish standing there with the axe in his hand. Susan's face was beaming, something that warmed his heart as much as the party itself.

"Daddy, Randy planned this almost all by himself! Can you believe that? He even helped Mama and me to make the cake and supper, too! It's your favorite, see?"

June was bubbling over with excitement and had put on her best dress for the occasion. Bob thought she looked beautiful and so grown up for thirteen. He smiled broadly.

"It's the best birthday in the whole world," he said quietly. He stooped over and put the axe against the wall and rubbed his face with his hands.

"Brother, did you all give me a scare!" He took a deep breath and smiled. He plopped down in his favorite chair and pulled the footstool up and propped his feet on it.

"Okay, the king awaits," he grinned, holding up one foot for the kids to pull off his boot.

They both fell onto him tickling him, and laughing heartily. Soon they tumbled out of the chair and onto the floor. Bob reached out and grabbed the foot of his squealing wife and pulled her down, too.

Husky was inside the cabin for the surprise, and sensed the excitement. He was jumping around the group and barking excitedly.

The family rolled and tumbled and laughed until their faces were wet with tears. It was the best, most rewarding laugh that they had had in a very long time. Randy's party idea had been a complete glorious success!

Chapter 5

It was the night of the hayride for the area young people. The kids were going from the school down the hill to where Bob and Susan Greyson's creek met the river. Then they would follow the road along the river and stop for a picnic after they crossed the bridge into Widow Watson's meadow. Susan and Bob had been asked to help chaperone, so Old Jack volunteered to stay with their kids.

They told Husky to stay close to home and help Old Jack keep an eye on things. He always entertained June and Randy with lots of old timer stores.

He had been in these mountains most of his life and had helped the Greysons build their cabin when they came here. The children were smaller then and Old Jack had really been lonely since his wife, Rachel, had died. It seemed like the children and Old Jack had something special between them and so Bob and Susan liked to invite the old gentleman over as often as possible.

The family had shared their joy of the Lord with Old Jack and had all been thrilled when he too accepted Jesus Christ as his Savior. They would never forget the tears running down his smiling rugged face that day.

He had never been to church with Rachel, and had never really understood the truths of the Gospel. He had not realized he could rest eternally in the salvation bought by Jesus when He died for the sins of every man. Now, he had peace and joy knowing that one day he would be with the Lord forever, and would be reunited with his wife, who he knew was also a believer. He had seen her read her Bible for years but had felt that was only for her...not for him. He knew now how wrong he had been.

When Bob and Susan left that evening, Old Jack and the children were all three standing arm in arm on the porch. The fireplace made a warm glow behind them in the doorway.

***

Bob and Susan took their mares that night. It had been quite a while since they had been riding together, and since Susan had felt more like herself lately, she had suggested it.

Bob had not told her about the goat or the big man. He did not want to stir her imagination any. He just felt the goat was destroyed by an angry mama bear. And the big man? Well, he was not quite sure where he came from.

The mares were feeling frisky that evening. It was just at dusk and the chill of the fall air felt good on Susan's face. I'm glad Bob agreed to ride out tonight, she thought. I've needed so badly to be with the forest again.

Maybe Bob was right about the Martin twins' accident. Everyone seems to agree that that is what it was. I have to believe it, too. And I simply will not think about that poor man who drowned over at the other village. It was just a strange, tragic coincidence, she told herself firmly.

They were supposed to meet the group at the school gym. Pete Greer always drove his wagon with the two white mules for the school hayrides. All the kids really loved that old fellow. In fact, everyone liked Pete. He did janitorial work at the school after he milked his twenty cows every night.

Some people did not know where he got the strength to do so much. He just loved the kids and would do anything for them. Some of these kids' parents went on hayrides with Pete when they were in school. Now he was like a granddaddy to everyone. There was an old mountain rumor that Pete and his baby brother were raised in the woods by wolves or bears or something. Pete would not talk about it and besides, he did not have a brother. Most people felt it was a rumor.

"My horse wants to run, Bob! Let's race!" They were only about a mile from the school, but the woods were so thick all around that one would never know there were people so near. Susan needed them and was eager for their company.

***

It was long after dark before the wagon reached Widow Watson's meadow. Everyone had sung and laughed until they were hoarse. Mary Martin and her husband, Tom, came along to help chaperone. Other than the twins, they did have their daughter Wilma. She was a sophomore in high school and they realized that life had to go on. They drew tremendous strength from the Lord, and talked freely about their sons.

Widow Watson and her neighbors had built three big campfires for the picnic, and their glows were a welcome sight. Susan was tired, and eagerly dismounted. She was ready to snuggle up with Bob by the fire. Everyone had brought a basket supper and blankets to sit on. And, as usual, Widow Watson had three big kettles of hot cocoa and lots of marshmallows to roast.

"Bob, this is really a wonderful place to live, isn't it? The people are grand and it's so beautiful. Let's eat…I'm famished," she exclaimed as she pulled him toward the fire. She was more cheerful than he had seen her in a long time, and he smiled good-naturedly as she tugged at his arm.

Later, after they had eaten and were sitting beside one of the campfires, Bob was remembering when they had built their stone fireplaces in the cabin. He had always loved the campfires and fireplaces, so their fireplace was the first thing to be completed. Then they had built their cabin around it. They so loved the first one that they had built another in their bedroom, and they enjoyed it just as much.

There was nothing like being outdoors with the cold night air and a big campfire to keep him and his Susan warm. She felt so soft leaning against his chest and her hair smelled clean and fresh.

"Mmmmm, nice," he said, giving her a squeeze.

The light of the fires and the full moon made it glow. He stared into the dancing flames while a warm feeling of contentment spread through him. Silently he thanked God that all was right again.

Most of the teenagers were off on their moonlight treasure hunt. They had to go in groups of four and each pair had a lantern or flashlight and a list of things to find. The time limit was one hour and they had been gone about twenty minutes.

Their lanterns off in the trees looked like so many fireflies, and the adults could hear the fun and giggles of anticipation in their voices.

It would have been grand to have grown up in this place, and Bob was thinking how glad he was that they had brought their children here to live. There was so much of nature, beauty, and love in a place like this. The people here had accepted the Greysons with warmth and kindness.

Bob's happy thoughts were erased suddenly when they all heard a piercing scream! They were on their feet immediately and with pounding hearts, began running toward the sound.

All the teenagers came quickly to see what was wrong. At first Wilma was so hysterical that no one could understand her. The boys with her tried to calm her as they blurted out what they knew.

"One minute Jill was here, and then she was gone!"

"Who did you say?" Mrs. Watson asked.

"Jill, Jill Clark," came the terrified reply.

"We all thought she was hiding and we kept laughing and looking for her. Then we got scared and got mad at her for hiding!"

"But she never answered us," Larry shuddered. "We've got to find her. She wasn't feeling very good and I'm scared."

"What's this?" Bob reached toward Wilma as she clutched something close to her.

"They…they're my brothers' bandannas…" she cried softly as she handed them to Bob.

He saw that there were two red bandannas knotted together. Each had the initials K.M. on them. He looked at Wilma and said, "They were wearing them the day they disappeared, weren't they?"

Mrs. Martin gasped and threw her hand to her mouth as her husband steadied her. With white faces they both moved toward Wilma and put their arms around her. She began to scream again and her terror put fear in all their hearts. "And now Jill is gone! Whoever took Kenny and Kelly took Jill! Oh, Mamaaaaa…." she sobbed as she buried her face in her mother's shoulder. She became so hysterical that she had to be carried back to the wagon to be taken home.

It was tragic enough to know the twins had had a terrible accident, but the suggestion that someone had taken them was beyond belief. There was silence among the people now. No one but Susan had really thought it

51

was more than an accident before, but now everyone was truly frightened that it might be. And what else could they believe since the bandannas were found at the place where Jill had disappeared.

***

The next morning was a cold gray day. The fog had lifted, but the fear in Joan Clark's heart had not. "She is only eighteen and is so beautiful," she said softly of her only child. "She hasn't been herself for weeks and now this. What is happening to her out there?" Jill's mother sat quietly on the fallen tree where the campfires had been the night before. The searchers had made this their headquarters and some women and parents from the village had been bringing steaming coffee and food during the night and early morning hours. Several women were silently making bacon and egg sandwiches for a fast breakfast for the searchers as they trickled in. Pastor Jordan had been called in and he had led prayers and was now out with the men searching for Jill. The atmosphere was quiet and somber and the happy singing voices from last night had disappeared.

No one answered Mrs. Clark's question, because no one knew the answer. Jill was a sweet, sensitive girl and most everyone liked her. She was quite a tomboy and loved horses and doing things with her father, Frank. She was an only child, and now her devoted father was out looking for her alongside her fiancé. He had tried to console Larry who kept blaming himself for her disappearance.

Frank had admired Larry during his childhood years. Growing up without a father seemed to have strengthened Larry's character rather than weaken it. Frank had often taken the Miller children fishing or hunting with him and Jill. It was only in the last couple of years that Jill and Larry had become attracted to one another. Larry's mother, Faye, as well as Frank and Joan Clark had been delighted when it became apparent that the pair would marry.

Larry had made quite a big affair of the proposal, even going so far as to ask Frank for her hand. It was all very romantic and everyone had been enjoying watching their courtship develop. Larry loved Jill deeply and they had a beautiful Christmas wedding planned.

Mary Martin sat beside Jill's mother, wringing the red bandannas in her hands. Everyone was now certain that something terrible must have happened to her little boys before they died.

Bob's thoughts kept returning to the day he ran out of gas by the river. Who was that big burly man? Why was he running wild in the forest? Or was he wild? He sure looked that way with his black bushy beard and ragged clothes. Even his eyes had a strange look about them. Could he have taken Jill? Did he take the twins?

Now he felt so stupid for having not told already. Bob decided it was time to tell the sheriff what he had seen that day only two weeks before. Grimly he went to find him.

***

Sheriff Billings was concerned about Bob's story of the big man. Was Bob sure of what he saw? Why didn't the man talk to Bob? Why didn't he tell anyone before now? Why did he have blood on him? No one else had reported seeing him. The sheriff decided they should not tell anyone else at this time for fear of a panic, at least until there was more information.

No one had found a sign of anything at the spot where Jill disappeared and everything else in the area seemed to be normal. It was only a few hundred yards to the river, so searchers went up and down on both sides for several miles and found nothing. Some people still had the hope that she had only gotten separated from the rest of the group, but then why had they not heard her calling, and why could they not find her now?

Chapter 6

It was dawn. The big man could see the morning sun coming over the mountain. The frost in the big trees made a beautiful shimmering reflection. The golden and amber leaves were falling gently in the breeze, and the air smelled good. The moisture from his breath froze in mid-air. The ice crystals sparkled in the morning sun.

Jill was warm and comfortable where she lay. She started to stretch and turn over, but the stabbing pain in her head kept her still. She looked around and could not remember where she was. It looked like a sort of cave, except there were bushes and brush around. Even some vines grew in along the rocky ceiling and walls. There was a smell of coffee in the air.

There was an old oak tree trunk that must have been three feet across. It had been cut to the height of a table. Its top was slick and shiny from years of use. A smaller trunk was nearby, obviously for use as a chair. Three large stacks of newspapers towered in the corner.

There were some candles on little rock shelves and over in a cool dark corner were some small mesh bags hanging from the ceiling of the cave. There were potatoes, onions, beets, carrots, radishes, and turnips in the bags. On the floor beneath the hanging bags were numerous different winter squashes. Near the front of the cave was an old metal milk can.

Jill could hear the dripping of water into the milk can from a spring near the top of the cave. The air was damp and cool but not cold. From where she lay, she could see a small amount of smoke going out of a hole in the ceiling. Her eyes followed the smoke downward to where there was a stove made from rocks and part of an old oil drum. There was an old kettle on the stove and she could smell coffee. A cast iron skillet hung from a peg on the wall and on a low narrow rock shelf there were some tin cups, old tin plates, and some spoons.

Jill became aware of the bed she was on. Animal hides cushioned her body and a big heavy quilt lay over her, with a large animal skin on top of that. She was just about to rise when she heard someone coming. She laid her arm across her face and pretended to be asleep. A big man parted the bushes and entered the cave.

He had a bag in one arm and a pile of firewood in the other. He stooped and laid the wood by the stove, and emptied the bag on the tree trunk table. There were wild berries, pears, apples, and nuts. Then he stepped outside and came right back in with a dead rabbit.

Jill watched secretly as the big man got a bucket of water out of the milk can. He sat on the stool and began dressing the rabbit. He saturated the hair in the water, then took his skinning knife and cut the head off with a swift stroke. Jill cringed as she watched the glimmering knife blade make a cut across the skin of the rabbit's back. He thrust both hands inside the cut and pulled the hide off opposite ends in two pieces.

Chapter 7

Susan's expert hands moved swiftly as she plucked the two big hens. It was the morning of Christmas Eve and she was preparing to fix chicken and dressing. She and June had gone into the woods and picked wild berries in the summer and had canned sauces and vegetables especially for this occasion. Old Jack was to come for Christmas dinner the next day and the spirit of Christmas was in the air. At least it was for those who could try and forget.

It had been three long months since Jill's disappearance and everyone had given up hopes of finding her. They had finally found one of her gloves with blood on it and had expected the worst. There had been extensive searches in and around Madison, but the single glove was the only clue. Everyone felt she would never be seen again. They tried to forget that this was the time when Jill and Larry were to have been married.

Wilma had never quite gotten over it, as Jill was her best friend. After losing her only brothers just weeks before, she withdrew into a shell. She would not talk to anyone and no one had been able to reach her.

Mary and Tom tried to hold their lives together, praying daily for their daughter Wilma. There was not much that was happy about the holiday season for them this year. Only the presence of the Lord kept them going. How they needed Him.

***

Randy and Bob had taken the mares into the forest to pick out a Christmas tree. There was snow everywhere and the forest was a glistening silver beauty.

Every branch was laden with snow and ice and bent under the weight.

Bob and Susan had decided to do all they could to make this a beautiful Christmas for their children in spite of the tragic months before. Bob and Randy sang heartily as they rode along, laughing at each other's mistakes. Every Christmas carol they could remember came to greet the sleeping forest.

They rode and rode, spending hours to find just the right tree. Finally, they found a perfect specimen and began the task of cutting it down. Bob had a heavy duty chain saw, but they had decided to go old-fashioned and each one had brought only an axe. Bob loved to chop wood that way. He could feel the pull of his muscles and felt his entire body warming. In spite of the cold temperature, he and Randy took off their coats and long red scarves while they worked. Susan had knitted them that summer so they that could have them in time for the cold winter months. They all needed to bundle up good, because they spent as much time outdoors as possible.

They got the tree ready and tied it to pull home with the horses. Then they sat down on a big snowy rock and opened the thermos Susan had sent. It was late, and they were deep into the forest. The ride home would take the rest of the day. The hot cocoa and thick ham sandwiches tasted delicious to them both. Bob had really learned to prefer sourdough bread on a sandwich rather than the store-bought kinds. And Pete's fresh milk cocoa was rich and warm. Randy commented how sweet and thick it was. His father agreed that it was especially good today. He said, "Your mother puts a lot of love into the things she sends us when we're out like this, doesn't she?"

"Yessir," Randy said around a mouthful of food. "Makes you feel like she is here with us all the time."

Then after swallowing, the boy smiled at Bob. "But Dad, I like for just us men to get away together sometimes. When Mama and June are along they do all the talking!" he laughed.

"You come in a good second," Bob replied with a grin, and reached over to ruffle his son's hair.

They sat in silence for a while, eating and enjoying their cocoa. Each thought his own thoughts. They were comfortable together even without conversation. While he chewed the thick ham slowly, Bob was absently gazing at an old huge pine tree. It had been struck by lightning two summers before. It had been leaning for some time and he noticed that it had finally fallen. It looked like a sleeping giant and he thought how sad it was that something that had been with the forest so long would never stand proud again. Then he noticed that where the dead roots had pulled loose from the frozen soil, there was a small baby tree. Only the little top showed above the snow. He was satisfied with the knowledge that there would again be life on that spot. He made a promise to himself that he would watch the growth of the new tree as years passed.

Randy finished eating first. He could put away enough food to feed three, Bob thought with a chuckle.

The boy went over to the horses to get their coats and scarves. It was beginning to feel chilly now that they were not active.

"Dad! Your scarf is gone! And here are some tracks in the snow. Looks like someone sneaked right up here and stole it!" Randy was clearly excited.

Bob thought how strange it was that anyone could be out there and he did not hear them. He walked around the mares and studied the tracks carefully. He noticed they were not very large and that the person had been wearing some kind of hiking boots.

"Let's follow the tracks, Daddy! Maybe we can find him!" Randy was eager and excited at the idea of a mysterious thief.

Bob knew they really did not have time to look round and still be home before dark, but he was curious himself and agreed.

"We can't go very far, but we will go look."

"Yippee!!" Randy dashed off following the path of tracks. He never thought of any danger, just of the fun he could have playing detective.

Bob was irritated at his carelessness and spoke sternly. "Randy! You just stop right there! We will stay together or we won't go, understood?"

"Yessir…I'm sorry, Daddy. I guess I got too excited. Do you think we will find him? Why do you think he took your scarf and not mine? Why didn't he take the horses, or our coats?"

"Whoa there, son! How many questions can I answer at one time anyway?" He laughed, to take the sting out of his reprimand. After all, this was Christmas and he did not want to have to discipline his children.

They walked along on either side of the trail. The tracks were double where the thief had returned in the same direction he had come. They did not have to go very far after all, because the trail ran out when the tracks led to the rocks by a stream which led to the river. They were slick and icy and left no prints. From where they stood, they could not see any more tracks anywhere. It was most disappointing.

"We had better head back, Son, and get that tree home to your mother," Bob said. They called and called trying to see someone in the forest, but to no avail.

"We might as well forget it. Whoever took it, did not take anything else, so he must have needed it." Bob thought about the big man but immediately discarded the idea. The tracks were much too small to be his.

"Rats!" exclaimed the disappointed boy. He would have liked to have spent the rest of the day looking for the mysterious scarf thief.

They mounted their horses, after gathering up their gear, and headed for home. They rode in silence for a while, and then Randy said, "Daddy, you don't think that whoever took the twins' bandannas took your scarf, do you?" Randy had been thinking how odd it was that Kelly and Kenny's bandannas had been found and then his daddy's scarf had been taken. He would like to think it might be a clue to the mysteries going on there on the mountain.

Bob did not know what he thought, but he did know it was Christmas Eve and he did not want anything to spoil their mood.

"Of course not, and anyway, who knows that there is anyone out there that would hurt anyone? Jill could have gotten lost and fallen into the river or something. And the twins themselves could have lost their bandannas."

"But, Dad…"

"Now, I don't want you to worry about it anymore. It was probably some kid out hiking that just wanted to play a trick on us. I bet we'll find out who it was someday!"

Then he began to sing, "Jingle bells, jingle bells…" He was determined to put the holiday spirit back into their day. Randy reluctantly joined in, and they headed off through the woods toward home.

Chapter 8

By dusk, when they rode into the yard with the tree, June had all the ornaments ready. They could smell pumpkin pies and fresh bread baking, and the aroma of coffee was deliciously inviting. They were both ready to get in and warm up by the fire and fill their stomachs again. It had been a long but enjoyable day for both Randy and Bob, in spite of the mystery of the scarf.

Since their move to Madison, Bob and Susan had made their own tradition of trimming their tree on Christmas Eve. When they lived in the city, they either used an artificial tree or a dried out real one and had it decorated weeks before Christmas. By Christmas Day, they were all sick of it and were happy to get it down!

Christmas had taken on a new meaning since the family had given their lives to the Lord Jesus. Bob looked forward to late evening when the family would gather 'round and he could read in the Scriptures the story of the birth of the baby Jesus.

Bob felt warm and satisfied sitting in his easy chair by the fire. He wiggled his toes as he stretched his bare feet toward the blaze. He thought his girls looked so wonderful buzzing around arranging and rearranging the tree ornaments.

"Daddy, PLEASE quit eating my popcorn strings!" June said with mock severity. At thirteen, she sure is a bossy little lady, Bob thought. Grinning, he swatted her with a stocking as she bustled over and swiped the popcorn from him. Christmas was a wonderful season for their family. I love everything about it, Bob thought.

"Hark! The herald angels sing…glory to the newborn King!" The voices came from outside the cabin. The Greysons all exchanged puzzled glances and rushed to the door.

What a wonderful sight! It was the same group of teenagers who had been on the hayride in the fall. No one expected them to go caroling this year after what had happened, and there was Pete, driving them around in his wagon. They all had lanterns and in their glow, the kids' faces looked like angels. It was mighty hard to believe anything bad could have ever happened around here, Bob thought.

In the lantern light Pete's long gray beard made him look like Santa, and Randy said so. The happy group of people laughed their "Ho! Ho! Ho's!" into the cold night air.

When they had all filled up on cocoa, the wagon pulled out of the yard and Pete yelled, "Hey, Randy! Merry Christmas to all, and to all a good night! Ho! Ho! Ho!"

The family watched the lights and listened to the sounds of Christmas as the wagon disappeared around the bend into the icy forest. It was beginning to snow as they stood there and the beautiful scene put a glow into their hearts.

***

Late that night, lying in their bed, Bob and Susan counted their blessings. They reminisced about their years together, the births of their two beloved children, and the changes that had come into their lives since moving to Madison. They were truly living and feeling the spirit of Christmas.

"Did you enjoy your day with Randy? What was all the chatter about your scarf? With all the excitement, I never quite got the whole story," Susan said, snuggling closer to Bob, enjoying the feel of his warm body next to hers.

"Well, it was really strange," he said, pulling her closer and getting comfortable. Someone sneaked up and took my scarf from the saddle while we were cutting the tree. We found his tracks and followed them, but they ran out when we got to the creek. I told Randy that whoever it was must have needed it because that was all he took."

"That's too bad! I worked all summer knitting those scarves. Who do you think it was?"

"I figured it was some kid pulling a prank or something, and I *know* how hard you worked! I love you for every stitch, too," he said, giving her a squeeze. "Anyway, maybe someone will have a better Christmas because of the scarf."

They said their bedtime prayers and especially thanked God for Christmas, the time to remember their precious Savior's birth. Then Bob kissed Susan gently and they lay in silence each thinking private thoughts. They went to sleep like that, as they had so many nights before.

Chapter 9

The gigantic tree had crashed through the roof of the cabin. The fire was engulfing everything, and the heat was unbearable. The flames roared up through the branches of the big tree like a forest fire! The horror was intense! "Where are you, Billy? Where are you? Andy! Andy! Please! Please!" Peter's screams were a frightened horrifying pleading.

"Peter! Oh, Peter! Get out!" Andy cried hoarsely. Then Peter was running, running! He had to get away. Still the flames followed. Everywhere he turned, he could see Andy's face, his mouth open in a silent scream. Still running…clouds of smoke engulfing his body, choking him with helpless horror. The horror of death. What could he do to help?

The fire was everywhere. Back in the cabin, Billy was pinned under the monstrous tree. Peter had seen him fall! And Andy was too young to die! But he was burning to death right this instant, and it was Peter's fault!

"Andy! Andy! Billy! Please…"

The smoke was overpowering Peter. Coughing and choking, he fell to the ground, his face buried in the snow. Tears of anguish and grief froze on his face.

"Oh, Dear God!" It was one last desperate plea.

Pete sat up straight in the bed. The sound of his own voice had awakened him. He took a breath of clean, fresh air to clear the smoke from his lungs. He knew it was only a dream, but he always felt choked afterwards.

He got up out of the bed in his stocking feet and went into his kitchen. He made a pot of coffee, and as he dressed he wondered if the dreams would ever stop. He had had them for years and never had they been more intense than now.

It was only four o'clock in the morning, but Pete knew he would never go be able to go back to sleep. He decided to stoke up the potbellied stove in his kitchen. The sound of the crackling fire was a soothing comfort in the early morning chill. He turned off the gas burner and set the coffee pot on the wood-burning stove. Then he pulled the old creaky rocking chair up by the fire and propped his feet on a stool. He had poured a big mug of coffee and cupped his calloused hands around it. "It's funny," he thought, "a nightmare about fire, and yet the blaze comforts me. In all the movies I see, anyone who has been in a fire is terrified of it."

Pete knew that the fire had been a turning point in his life. He had always blamed himself for Andy's death, because if he had not brought the boy to the mountain, he would not have died in the fire. He did not really feel at fault for the death of Billy, but he did feel great remorse for the old trapper had been so good to him and Andy.

They had made a crash landing during a wind and snow storm on the mountain that winter. Miraculously, Pete and Andy were unharmed. They were trapped in the small airplane, though, and were near freezing and starvation when Billy found them. They had managed to swallow some snow they could reach through a window and they had carried a few candy bars and nuts which they later decided had helped to save their lives.

They had lost count of the long days and nights after the crash. One day, about mid-day, Billy found them. He had been out hunting a wounded fox and had stumbled upon the small plane in the snow.

He could tell it had been there awhile, because there was deep snow on it and was drifted around the body and wings. He had not been sure what it was at first and he began to poke around, mostly out of curiosity.

66

The grizzled old trapper was extremely startled when he heard their muffled voices coming from under the snow. They had heard him mumbling to himself, and could hear his movements on the outside. They had looked at each other in complete disbelief, then began shouting and laughing. They both cried as they laughed with the joy of the discovery that they had come to believe was never going to happen.

Billy had taken them to his cabin and had cared for them until the night of the awful fire. Pete knew that he never would forget that old man and his kindness, and he knew the dreams would never let him forget the sight of the old trapper pinned beneath the pine tree. Neither would he ever forget the brutal fire that killed both his friends. Pete had decided to settle in the mountains and never go back to his old life. The events that followed the fire were the deciding factors in his decision to stay in the wilderness.

One of the first things he did after the initial shock of the fire was to build himself a shelter. He was twenty-five years old then and a strong figure of a man.

He never went back to Billy's old cabin site, but he remembered how the cabin had been made and kept those memories for future reference. His first shelter he made by using many branches and leaves from the forest. He had learned before the fire where Billy's traps had been set out, and he kept a vigilant watch on them and relied heavily on them for his food.

He also knew where Billy had kept his "stash" hidden away from bears and other scavengers, and he used it to store his own meats. There was a good supply of other food types there, also and Pete had a good steady diet for the rest of the winter. Peter had a lot of time to think during those long, cold weeks that followed. He grieved deeply for the loss of his young friend and never had the inclination to go back to the plane for the painful reminders that he knew were there. He eventually came to the conclusion that maybe this was where he ought to be living anyway. He decided that it was some stroke of fate that had brought him here and he knew that this was where he belonged. He had no family and no other reason to go back to his old life.

That spring, he had ventured down the mountains on week long hikes and before long he met other loners in the area and was known to them as "Pete" rather than his given name, Peter.

By wintertime he and some of the others had moved on down into the valley and become a part of the village of Madison.

***

Pete did not like to remember his dreams so he turned his thoughts to Christmas. This was Christmas Day and he had his plans to think about. Energetically, he slipped into his warm barn clothes and hurriedly went out to milk his cows.

Christmas was an especially wonderful time for Pete. He loved to do for others things that were never done for him before he came here. He had grown up in a mid-western city in an extremely poor family. His mother died when he was ten years old, and he was raised by his father and grandmother. They lived in the ancient family homestead. Christmas was special then too, but they had hardly enough to get by. His grandmother had a way of making something out of nothing, and after she and his father were killed in an auto crash when he was twenty, he tried to carry on his life with the training he had received. His nature was to give, and he was going to make Christmas special for someone who needed it most.

68

He had made special plans to help his friends, Tom and Mary Martin and Wilma enjoy their day, but they did not know it yet. He chuckled with anticipation as he whisked back into the warm kitchen, the smell of barn on him. As he hung the barn clothes in a closet near the door, he thought how this Christmas was so full of sadness for the Martins, and he intended to do something about that.

Pete had left his coffee cup warming on the wood stove. Now, he emptied it in one big noisy gulp, and began preparing his breakfast, He was a hearty eater and fixed bacon, eggs, pancakes with sorghum syrup, and more hot, black coffee.

Cooking was one of his pleasures and he poured a tall glass of ice cold milk as he moved around the kitchen. It was fresh and creamy, just milked the night before. He always kept a jug in the coldest part of the refrigerator. Visitors really enjoyed Pete's sweet milk. Nearly everyone in the village brought their jugs two or three times weekly. Pete filled them from a spout on the giant vat which mixed and chilled the fresh milk. He managed to make a good living with his milk cows and he worked at the schoolhouse so he could be near the children. The money he earned at that job went into the bank and he had a sizeable savings. It was at special times like Christmas that he dipped into that bank account. As he had no family, he enjoyed sharing his life with the people of the village.

When Pete had eaten breakfast, just after daybreak, he heard the sound of hoof-beats. He knew it would be Old Jack on his favorite buckskin. Their plans that morning would keep them both busy until Old Jack would go to the Greyson's cabin for Christmas dinner. Pete opened the door with a jerk and the burst of cold air made him shiver.

"Come on in here, old timer!"

"Old timer, huh? You are just a young whippersnapper your ownself!" Old Jack laughed heartily and stomped the snow from his boots before going in. He was in his sixties and Pete was about ten years his junior. They always enjoyed fussing about their ages. Pete's gray beard gave him the appearance of being older, and Old Jack was spry and extremely youthful. They were both very active and had become fast friends over the years.

As Jack hung up his coat, cap, and scarf, Pete said, "Well, partner, you ready to get these baskets finished and delivered?"

"You bet your boots I am! This is some of the most fun about Christmas! Where are the bows from the flower shop?"

"Over on that table in the corner. Do you want a cup of hot coffee to warm your innards?" Pete went into the warm kitchen to pour their coffee. The good smell of bacon still lingered in the air. He knew Jack would want his coffee black and steaming.

"You might as well bring a coupla baskets in to the kitchen table. I'll get more fruit set out," he called to Jack.

It did not take the men long to arrange the fruit and nuts into the baskets. A few little toys went into the baskets which would go the families with small children. They swiftly tied the cellophane and colored ribbons onto the fruit baskets. After about a dozen baskets, they were finished. They had done the others the day before.

They talked of the excitement of the day as they worked. Then a little sadness came into their mood when Pete mentioned how lonely Wilma Martin had looked the night before. In his heart, he was reminded of the lonely teenage boy who had died in the fire so many years before. He determinedly shook the thought from his

70

mind, and in a few moments, he and Old Jack prayed together for the Lord to help Wilma and to heal her hurt.

"Well, I for one, am not gonna let the Martin's Christmas be spoiled!" Pete exclaimed.

"What are you planning to do, Pete?" Old Jack wondered what they could do to help ease their sorrow. When he lost his Rachel a few years back, he felt like he would never be happy again. He was so lonely and empty and felt so useless. It was not until the Greysons moved close and became his friends, and introduced him to Jesus, that he began to love life again. His friendship with Pete had grown immensely as the two Christian men shared their lives with the community. Living a God-centered life had served to accentuate Pete's giving nature, and Old Jack found it to be quite contagious.

Grinning broadly, with his hands on his hips, he asked with a chuckle. "Whatcha got up your sleeve this time?"

"Well, for one thing, the Martin family is gonna help us deliver these baskets to people around here. Seeing their bright happy faces ought to cheer them up!"

Chapter 10

The little pine tree looks beautiful, she thought. She had decorated it with holly berries and bright colored bird feathers. She had made some bells and balls from tin foil, then had cut a star from paper and covered it with the foil, too. She had just placed it at the top of the little tree and was standing back admiring it.

Jill had put several candles around the tree on the tree-trunk table and the glow of their flames made it the most beautiful tree ever. She had neatly folded the red knitted scarf on the table beside the tree. She was so proud to have something else to give Uncle Andrew. She had used his hunting knife and carved him a beautiful statue of himself. Every loving detail was carefully carved. It was only six inches tall but was a good likeness. The little statue had broad shoulders, big arms, and wore only ragged pants. That was the way he had looked the first time she saw him. The face was almost hidden by the beard and long hair.

Jill was never afraid of him. He was so very gentle from the beginning. He told her that he had found her in the woods where she had fallen and hit her head. He had tended her wound so gently and had spoon-fed her with soup until she was strong enough to eat alone. They had not talked much the first few days. Jill had been too weak and very nauseated and sick most of the time. There were times when Andrew thought he might have to find a doctor for her. She assured him, though, that it was not necessary.

Before long, he began to talk to her. He was a very lonely man, and something about her made him talk about things he had chosen long ago to forget. She told him that she could not remember anything from before her fall, and that he was all she had in the world. His kindness and gentleness had been proof enough that he was a good person. She asked him once why he lived out in the woods all alone, and where his family was.

"I guess, Little One, that these woods are my family. Oh, I can remember someone who was supposed to be related to me. I was just a boy then. My parents died in an epidemic and I was placed in the home of an aunt and uncle. They had seven children already, and I guess they didn't have time to really love me. Sometimes they beat me and put me in a closet for punishment. I could never understand why they never put their kids in there. Finally, they got tired of me and sent me to an orphanage. They said they just couldn't afford the extra expense. I knew it was just because they didn't like me. I was big for my age and was very clumsy. I was always breaking things by accident. They said I was rebellious. They even had everyone in the neighborhood thinking I was a troublemaker, when all I wanted was a friend."

Jill had felt great compassion that cool evening as they had sat outside the cave. She thought that maybe this was a place where she was really needed.

"Andrew, do you care if I call you 'Uncle' Andrew? I can be your family. I need you too, you know, because I don't have anyone either."

Andrew had been touched as he looked deeply into her blue eyes. Putting his big hand on her shoulder, he said softly, "I would be proud to have you for my family, Little One," and big tears made their way down his face into the bushy black beard.

"I'm sorry, Uncle Andrew. I didn't mean to hurt you…please don't cry."

Jill's eyes pooled with tears as she saw the deep pain he felt. "It's not you, Little One. This just makes me remember someone I did love once. And he really loved me, I think. He was like a brother to me, and he died…oh, how that hurt! I wish you could have known him," the big man said, wiping his eyes with the back of his hand.

After that day, Jill and Andrew became as family and swore their loyalty to one another.

***

Jill went to the old milk can and dipped enough water to make a fresh pot of coffee. She knew Uncle Andrew would be back soon, chilled to the bone. He was out making exchanges today. He did that once or twice a week.

He had taught her to roast birds over the fire and she had been roasting a young, fat turkey all morning. She also had made pan bread on top of the stove and had yams covered in tin foil baking in the open fire outside.

The calendar on the wall of the cave showed that today was Christmas and Jill's excitement filled the air with song. She was singing joyously as she worked and was only slightly startled when she turned, with two plates in hand, and saw Uncle Andrew standing there watching.

"Oh, Uncle! Are you trying to scare the daylights out of me? You can move as quiet as a mouse!" she exclaimed, with playful surprise.

"Well?" she set the plates down, put her hands on her hips, and looked around waiting for his reaction to her decorations.

Andrew's eyes filled with tears as he looked all around the cave. It had been such a long time since he had shared Christmas with anyone.

"Looks like a party, Little One! How long have you been planning this?" He was overjoyed, that was plain to see, and it almost made Jill cry, too, to see how happy he was. She threw her arms around him and gave him a quick squeeze.

"Long enough to pull it off!" she said, swallowing a lump in her throat. She pulled him on into the cave and began to chatter happily.

"Come and see the little tree. Remember the feathers you saved last summer? I used them on it. Don't they look beautiful with the holly berries?" she said excitedly.

"That is the most beautiful tree in the world, Little One! Thank you! You've made this the best Christmas I ever remember!" He moved over to the tree. "What's this? A statue? Why, it looks like me!"

"It *is* you, silly! Do you like it?" Jill was thrilled at his reaction, and smiled with delight, twisting her shoulders from side to side as she watched him.

"So, that's what you were carving all those weeks! Where did you ever learn to do that?" He glanced suddenly at her, knowing the discomfort she felt at the mention of her lost past.

"It's okay, Uncle Andrew. I don't really remember, but it came naturally to me. Did you see the scarf?"

She had lied to him again and she liked it less and less. She had lied to Andrew from the start and every time she did it now, it seemed to stab her heart from the inside. She had to change the subject, to keep from blurting out her secret. It was like a hard knot in the midst of her being. She knew that it would have to be soon, but not now. Not now.

She picked up the scarf, and unfolding it, she draped it around his thick neck. She stood on tip-toe and he still had to bend down to accept the gift. He kissed her on the forehead, thanking her, and his bushy black beard tickled her nose.

"It's beautiful," he said quietly, taking her by the hand. He led her outside to where he had tied a lovely black pony. It was sleek and shiny with long, graceful legs.

"Oh, Uncle Andrew!" she shrieked. "For me? Wherever did you get him?"

There was a new black saddle with silver decorations on it to match the bridle. The horse nuzzled Jill when she walked around to stroke the saddle.

Now it was her turn to cry. She said no more but laid her face against the horse's warm neck and shed tears that she had held back for such a long time.

Andy stood by, waiting, relieved to see her crying; truly crying, from deep inside. She had kept so much inside all along. She had been very happy with Andrew, but he knew she must hurt deeply when she thought about her lost past. How devastating it would be to have no memory. His heart ached for her loss.

After a while, she raised her head, sniffling. "I love him, Uncle Andrew. He is so very beautiful! Thank you so much… but how did you ever manage to trade for a horse?"

"Now, Little One, don't you fret about that. It's Christmas! Well? Are you going to ride him?" He did not like to see the child worry.

"Oh, yes! Come on, Ebony! Let's go!" She jumped onto his back and grinned at Andy. "It's the perfect name, don't you think?" Laughing from deep within, she pulled the reins and galloped off down the trail, the snow flying behind.

***

Someday, she will have to go back, he thought, then quickly turned away. He went over to the fire where the turkey was browning and checked on the yams he could see there in the hot coals.

He thought how lucky he was to have known the companionship of this young person. The relationship had been very rewarding, and had given him more ambition. He was going closer and closer to villages than ever before on the days when he went out to make exchanges as he called it. He was not sure she would understand if she knew he "made exchanges" without the knowledge of some of his "customers". He did not really feel like it was stealing, because he always left something in place of the item he took. And sometimes people who lived away from a village would let him cut firewood or do other chores in exchange for goods or food. Some people even left items out in a special place and he would take them, leaving something in return. It seemed that those people enjoyed the mystery of exchanges. Those who did not tolerated it because he never took much. He was rarely seen by people who made secret exchanges, willingly or not, and he seemed reserved and quiet to the few people who saw him.

He had become quite friendly with only one person, but she had died years ago. The people who saw him knew he lived somewhere in the wilderness because no one in the villages ever mentioned him.

Before long, Jill came riding back to camp, breathless and exhilarated. Her cheeks were flushed from the cold and her hands were icy. She had rushed off without any extra wrap besides her bulky sweatshirt, and was anxious to get warm by the fire.

Andy had the turkey partially carved and their plates filled when she came back.

"Oh, that was fantastic!" she cried. This has to be the happiest Christmas ever!" She rubbed her hands briskly, chattering excitedly. It was one of the things he enjoyed about her. She could talk for hours and totally and happily entertain him.

77

"Are you hungry, Little One? You put out quite a feast today!"

She really had not had a good appetite lately, but this was Christmas and she did not want him to be concerned about her.

"Yes, I sure am! I could eat a whole turkey…but then there wouldn't be enough for you!" She moved past where he sat with his plate and patted him on the head.

Chapter 11

It had not taken Old Jack and Pete long to convince Tom and Mary to come along with them. They felt like it would be good for Wilma, and besides, they needed to get out. It was their first Christmas without the twins.

Mary had been relieved to hear the bells announcing the arrival of someone that morning. She felt her spirit perk up, as she had been so down-hearted about Christmas this year. It seemed all she could think of was last Christmas.

***

The twins and Wilma had made up a wonderful surprise for her. They had secretly saved all summer to buy her a new sewing machine for Christmas. She remembered how she had made the twins their red flannel shirts on her old machine and how it kept quitting. She had worked endless hours on that old thing, trying to finish the shirts for Christmas. She stayed up late at night, working and worrying how she was ever going to finish them in time.

The red velvet dress she was making for Wilma seemed impossible to finish because the old machine seemed to want to "eat" the material every time she sewed on it. And she had been so determined to give them all to her children by Christmas Eve so they could wear them on Christmas Day. She remembered how, about a week before Christmas, she had gone in tears to the Widow Watson for help. The kind old lady had allowed her to use her machine in spite of the fact that she used it every day doing alterations for the villagers. She made clothes for many of the children and was able to make a living at what she earned. Mary remembered how Widow Watson had comforted her, offering her a hot cup of lemon tea and a shoulder to cry on. She had felt so desperate, and had been quite anxious to finish on time. Well, she did, thanks to Widow Watson, and on Christmas Eve she joyously gave her children their new clothes. They were all appreciative and rewarded her labors with hugs and kisses. Then they all gave her their gifts. Kenny had a small box all wrapped in silver with red ribbon, and when she opened it there were two spools of thread. She thought about what an odd gift it was, but she knew that one could never tell about a ten year old boy.

Then Kelly had given his gift to her. It was a little larger and was wrapped in blue paper with gold ribbon. It was funny how she could remember even the tiniest details about that night. Kelly's package had a yard of yellow and brown material in it. By this time, Mary began to get a little suspicious. When she saw the gift that Wilma had, she felt her heart beating faster, and could not wait to open it. It was a much larger box, and she just knew it was the right size for a sewing machine! She was already wondering how on earth the kids managed to do this, as she ripped the paper off the package. But then, when she opened it, there was another box inside, all wrapped in colorful Christmas paper. So she looked quizzically at Wilma and laughed, opening the next box. Inside, she found another box, and still another, until there was one tiny box in the bottom. Well, by now, she had decided they had bought a ring or something, and that the thread and material had been to throw her off track. Her heart sank, though she tried to act thrilled as she opened the tiny box. But when she opened it, there was nothing in it but a folded piece of paper. When she looked, all three children were on the floor beside her, on their knees, leaning forward with anticipation.

"Well, open it Mama!" The twins were so excited that they were giggling and bouncing around.

Mary hurriedly opened the piece of paper. It had a neatly printed message, which she knew had been written by Kelly because of the circles over the I's. It said,

"Because you are so special,
and our new clothes are red,
Your real gift is waiting
at the foot of your bed!
We love you!
Kenny, Kelly and Wilma"

"How did you know you were getting clothes, and how did you know they were red?" she called as she rushed into the bedroom. At first, she did not see anything there except the cedar chest in which she kept her quilts. When she doubtfully jerked the lid up and saw the shiny new Singer machine, she burst into delighted tears and let the lid fall as she grabbed all three of the children in her arms. They were all laughing and crying at the same time, knowing one another's feelings. Tom had stood leaning on the door frame with his arms crossed and a tender smile on his rugged face.

***

The tears were flowing down Mary's face that morning when she heard the bells on Pete's horses as they pulled up to the house. Soon, they were all loaded into the wagon among the bright colored baskets. The two white mules blew vapor from their nostrils as they started out in the cold crisp morning.

Old Jack had fastened the leather straps with bells onto the harnesses. The bells jingled merrily as they rode along and announced their arrival to each house as they approached.

After a while, they began making some stops in the country. They arrived at Widow Watson's small cottage about ten o'clock that morning. She invited them all in for hot coffee or cocoa, thanked them for her basket, and cheerfully sent them on their way.

The morning went fast and soon it was time to take Old Jack back to Pete's house so he could go on over to the Greyson's for Christmas dinner.

When they pulled the wagon up to Pete's, Old Jack said, "I'll just tie Bucky up behind the wagon and you all come on over to Bob's with me. We can deliver their basket together."

"That's a good idea, Jack. Tom, you don't mind riding out there, do ya?" Pete asked, sensing what Old Jack had in mind.

They rode along in silence, except for the jingle of the bell straps. The fresh snow from the night before made the forest look beautiful. Pete noticed some fresh tracks on the roadside where someone had been out on horseback that morning.

It was cloudy and cold. Tiny flakes of snow were beginning to fall as they rode along.

"Looks like we might get some more snow," Tom commented. Mary put her arm across Wilma's shoulders and smiled at Tom.

"It is really nice to be out today. Pete, I'm so glad you insisted we come. We are all having such a good time, aren't we, Honey?" Lovingly, she smiled at Wilma and gave her a squeeze. Much to her delight, Wilma smiled back at her.

***

Wilma had been thinking all morning about the last few months and how desperately sad she had felt. Something about the holiday made her feel selfish and she had acted so miserable. After all, her mother had lost enough when the twins died. Maybe it was her place to be more helpful to her mother. And maybe she could somehow even help Jill's poor mother. After all, Jill had

82

been her only child. Oh, Lord Jesus, she prayed silently, please forgive me and help me to forget.

"There are June and Randy! Oh, look what a wonderful snowman they are making!" The sound of Wilma's excited voice startled everyone, even June and Randy heard her shout. They had seen the wagon coming around the bend, but they had already heard the bells before it came into view. They were waving and yelling to the smiling group in the wagon. Both of them could see the change in Wilma and were exhilarated and excited. They knew it had been a long hard adjustment for the Martin family.

Bob had been watching for Old Jack and had just stepped up to the picture window when all the excitement started.

"Susan, come see what is happening!" he called to her as he grabbed a coat and ran outside.

Susan could not imagine what was causing all this activity! She had been making a last minute centerpiece for their Christmas table. It had pinecones and holly with berries, and she had arranged it all in a wreath of pine boughs. She was fastening on the last tiny pine cone when the racket started. She still had it and the bright red bow in her hand as she rushed onto the porch.

"Oh, Pete! What a wonderful surprise! We didn't expect to see you today! And Tom and Mary! Well, climb down from there, you all look frozen!" Susan was as thrilled to see the group of callers as she had been with Christmas itself.

June had run around to the side of the wagon where Wilma was holding their Christmas basket out to her. Their eyes met for a brief moment of understanding as June took the colorful basket from Wilma's hands. They both smiled and were talking all at once like everyone else.

For just an instant, Randy felt a twinge of loneliness for his twin friends who were not here today. Then he rallied and began chattering gaily to the big white mules. "How ya doin' ole boys? Merry Christmas to ya both!" he said in a hearty, husky voice.

Everyone laughed, and suddenly it seemed as if this Christmas was going to be a happy one after all.

"Wilma, come on and help us finish our snowman!" Randy said excitedly as he took her by the hand and led her away. He could not believe she had a sparkle in her eyes and not that sad, far-away gaze that they had all become so accustomed to.

The adults went on into the house, laughing and talking. Susan told everyone that they simply had to stay for Christmas dinner.

"I always cook far too much anyway," she said to convince them. And, it did not take much convincing as Old Jack had known she would insist they stay. He knew one way to help Pete make a good day for the Martins would be to give them some companionship and love.

Pete had a warm contented feeling deep inside as he could already see the healing work God was doing in Wilma's shattered life. He lingered a moment watching her and the Greyson children laughing and throwing snow at one another. Then, as he followed the others inside, he thought, the Lord does indeed answer prayers. With a smile and a chuckle, he closed the door behind him.

Chapter 12

Later that same afternoon, Jerry Davis came riding up to the Greysons' cabin. "Hello? Anybody here?" He called out, his naturally red face crimson with excitement. He did not get down from his horse, but waited anxiously for the family to come outside.

Almost immediately, the door opened, and Bob came out. "Well, Merry Christmas, Jerry! Whatever brings you out this way?"

"Hi! I have been looking for Bonnie. She's my brother's girl…they're visiting for Christmas. Anyway, we gave her a horse and a saddle and she went riding about two hours ago. She hasn't come back, so we started looking for her. Have you seen her? She is blonde and about twelve years old. Her horse is black with a saddle that's black and silver."

"Well, no, Jerry, we haven't been away from the cabin all day, and she hasn't been by that I know of. Wait a minute, and I'll ask Pete and Old Jack if they saw her on their way over this morning."

Then Bob insisted that Jerry come inside for some eggnog. After a few minutes of Christmas greeting from the happy group inside, Jerry found out that they had seen tracks beside the road, but had seen no one on horseback.

"Would you like for us to bring our horses and help you look for her? I bet she went into the woods and lost track of time…or maybe *she* got lost, being new here, and all!"

***

The lighthearted tone of his voice did not reveal dread in Bob's heart. The thought of having to search for another missing child was unbearable. What was becoming of their peaceful little town anyway, he asked himself. He prayed that this would be a false alarm and that they would find the little girl not far away and having a wonderful time on her new horse.

Bob and Randy went out to saddle the mares, and Old Jack got Bucky ready. Earlier they had unsaddled him and put him in the corral with fresh hay.

The big horse nuzzled his shoulder as he reached for the bridle. "Bucky, we have to help find a little girl. Ready?" Silently he prayed that they would find her alive and well.

Pete said he would take the wagon along and search the roads. He could watch for her and would signal with Bob's shotgun if he found her.

Mary and Susan looked at one another in silence, each knowing what the other feared. The two mothers prepared some sandwiches for the men, and got their warm clothing ready to go.

Within a few minutes, the group of searchers was ready to leave. They all mounted their horses, Tom Martin climbing up into the wagon with Pete. The women and girls stood outside the cabin watching as the men rode silently away.

"Come on, now…we'll find her! You wait and see!" It was Old Jack, forever optimistic, in spite of the tragedies that seemed to have beset their community.

They trotted off down the snow-packed road, with plans of where each would go and how to signal.

In less than half an hour, the three shots rang out in the cold still air!

"Oh, thank God they have found her!" Mary was so relieved that she began to sob. The anxiety of long futile searching for her small sons was still an open wound in her heart. Wilma and Susan moved to her side and placed their arms around her. June started to laugh shakily.

"We all act like a bunch of spooks, don't we? We just have to have a little faith! Bad things just DON'T happen on Christmas!"

They all laughed then, and went into the kitchen to celebrate with some more eggnog and fruitcake. They put on a big pot of coffee for the men, who would be coming back very soon.

***

But June was wrong. They had found her all right. It was Randy and Jerry who saw her lying there in the woods. They were shocked to see the pool of blood, crimson red against the brilliant white snow. Her head was lying in the bloody snow, and her beautiful blonde hair was matted with it. She was mumbling, and crying. It was nearly impossible to make out what she was saying.

Jerry made the signal with his rifle that he carried on the saddle with him. He hurriedly got off the horse, and with a stifled sob, rushed to Bonnie's side.

"Don't try to talk, Baby, you'll be alright. Just lie still."

He took off his heavy coat and laid it over her. He began to rub her hands to warm them. She still had on her gloves, but when he removed them, her little hands were icy. The blood was oozing from the gash in her head and Jerry wrapped it with his neckerchief.

Randy stood by helplessly, not believing what was happening. The only thing he knew to do was to go watch for the others and get Pete to bring his wagon so they could get her into the clinic. Doctor Jamison lived upstairs and was always home on Christmas as his mother from Omaha came for the holidays each year.

Randy mumbled to himself, "I bet Bonnie's folks are gonna wish they had *never* come to this place…" He miserably wiped his face with the back of his coat sleeve.

Shortly, he could hear the horses making their way toward him. They were on the trail, and he ran out to meet them.

"Daddy, she is back there, in the woods. She's hurt. Hurry! Where's Pete with the wagon?" Randy was near hysteria.

"Son, you take my horse and go get him. He was going back to the house. We never thought she would be hurt." Bob climbed down, relieved that the horse had only thrown her and nothing more tragic or mysterious had happened.

"Randy," he called. "How bad is she?"

"I don't know, but her head is bleeding! It looks awful!" Randy's face was pale, as he reined the mare and tried not to hurry her on the icy road.

"My horse… Mama? That awful man… Mama? He hit me… He was so big… he scared me… Mama? Where's Mama?" Bonnie was incoherent but Jerry latched onto something she said.

"Honey, did you say someone hit you? Bonnie, did someone hurt you?" Jerry was beginning to get very angry and was feeling confused. "What happened? Can you tell me, Sugar?" Part of him knew that she should not try to talk, but if someone had done this to her, then he wanted to know. "Bonnie?"

"My horse…he chased my horse away…Mama? Where's my horse?" Then the child became limp and still.

Shortly, the wagon arrived and they carefully laid her in the back. Jerry rode with her, still rubbing her hands. The horsemen rode alongside the wagon.

"Listen, Tom, I don't know exactly what happened back there," Jerry said nervously,

"But she said some man hit her and took her horse. It don't make any sense, but we've got to find him!"

As he firmly held the reins, Pete said, "Bob, why don't you and Old Jack take Randy and tell the doc we're coming? Me and Tom will be right along in the wagon!"

"Sure," Bob agreed, "and then we'll go over to Sheriff Billings and tell him what has happened."

Within half an hour, the sheriff had the whole story, and he capably took complete control of the situation.

"You men come with me and show me where this happened. I'll need your help in tracking the horse, and maybe that will lead us to the man, whoever it is!" The officer got into the police car with his deputy, and they drove off following the men on horseback just ahead.

They met another car that stopped in the road asking where the doctor lived. It seemed that the man and woman in the car were Bonnie's parents. They'd gotten word of the incident and were terrified for their daughter.

Old Jack and Randy went back to the cabin to tell Mary and the others what had happened. As they rode along, Randy broke the silence.

"Old Jack, what do you think happened to her? Why would a man hit a little girl and take her horse?"

"I don't rightly know, boy, but they'll find him…no one is going to do that around here and get away with it! I'll bet when they do find him, we will find out what happened to Jill and the twins, too!"

Randy looked quickly at him, "Oh?" he said in surprise.

As they rode up to the cabin, the ladies came out to greet them. Wearing big smiles and laughing, they were surprised to see the grim faces of the riders.

"What's wrong?" It was June who spoke first.

Wilma put her hand to her mouth, biting down hard on her knuckles. The two mothers were afraid to ask, and were not sure they wanted to know. They looked at each other, joining hands in dread.

"Well, we found her, but she had been hurt. It looked like someone hit her and took her horse. She seems to be hurt really bad." Old Jack could hardly bear to tell these mothers another bit of bad news. It seemed that bad news was all that they had heard lately.

"Where is she now? Did they take her to Doc?" Susan was overwhelmed by the news. "What do you mean someone *hit* her? I can't believe that! Surely the horse just threw her and she was hurt when she fell?"

Old Jack got down off Bucky and handed the reins to Randy. He went over to the ladies and said, "I'm sorry, but it looks like someone did it. The little girl said an awful man hit her and chased her horse away. She took a terrible blow to the head."

"Where are Tom and Bob?" Mary asked.

"They went ahead to tell the doctor and then to tell the sheriff. I imagine they will try to track the horse since it is still a couple of hours until dark." Old Jack took his handkerchief from his pocket and wiped his face, shaking his head in wonder.

The phone rang inside, and Susan ran to answer it. "Is it true? Did another child get hurt?" The sobbing voice on the line was familiar, but Susan could not quite recognize it.

"Yes, who is this? Are you alright?"

"It's Joan Clark, Jill's mother. What has happened? Who has disappeared this time?" She was crying through bitter tears, the fear returning for the unknown fate of her own child.

"Oh, Joan, it is Jerry Davis' niece, visiting for Christmas. She was riding her horse and had an accident.

We don't know exactly what happened yet. She has been taken to see Doc Jamison. I am sure she will be alright," Susan said tenderly to the distraught woman. "Joan, would you like for someone to come over and be with you? You sound very upset."

"No, that's alright, Frank is here, and besides, I'm getting used to being alone," she said bitterly.

"Please, Joan, we might be able to help if we come over. Mary Martin is here with me, and we could come right away." Susan could not bear to have her friend so broken hearted, and though she knew only time could erase the pain, she still wanted to help.

"Alright, Susan," Joan stifled a sob, and gave in to Susan's urging. "Thanks, I guess I really could use some company right now, Frank has been awfully upset, and I don't know what we're going to do." She sniffed and said bravely, "I'll get a pot of coffee on and will see you in a few minutes then."

Wilma had heard enough to know what was happening and said, "Can June and I go, too? She was a dear friend to me when Jill and I were…" She turned away, unable to finish.

Cheerfully Susan replied, "Sure, come on! We could all use some fresh air. Just let me leave a note for Bob so they will know where we have gone." Susan did not feel very cheerful, though, knowing that someone had deliberately harmed a twelve-year-old child. She had not lied to Joan, but had not had the heart to tell her what they knew.

Silently she repeated Isaiah 41:10. "Fear thou not; for I am with thee…"

Chapter 13

It was late evening of Christmas Day. Jill had been inside the cave, lying on her animal skin bed. She had not felt well since the vigorous ride she had taken earlier when Uncle Andrew brought her the beautiful horse. She had not told him, however, and had just said she was tired and wanted a nap. She was beginning to realize that she would have to tell him soon what was really wrong with her. She also knew that she could not lie to him much longer about her past.

She sat on the edge of the bed, wondering where Uncle Andrew was. He had gone for a walk earlier, and she did not know if he had returned. She looked toward the wood stove and knew it would need to be fed. She went over to it, rebuilt the fire, and began to prepare some hot chocolate.

In a few minutes, she went to the entrance of the cave and looked outside. Uncle Andrew sat on a big log watching the horse eating some hay he had brought back for it. Jill was distressed to see that the big man seemed to be almost in tears. It had started to snow, and the flakes settled in his black hair, looking like shiny stars in the night sky.

"Uncle Andrew, what is it?" Jill went over to him and put her hand on his slumped shoulder.

"Oh, Little One, are you rested? I didn't want to wake you." He sniffed and tried to smile at her. She meant so very much to him and he did not like to concern her.

"Yes, I had a very nice nap. Now whatever is the matter? You looked so sad when I came out."

"Well, it was just that I was remembering something very painful. I had a pet once, not long ago…she was killed by a mama bear just this fall. I was just thinking I might have avoided that if I had made a pen for her so she wouldn't have wandered away," he paused for a minute, blinking his eyes. "You see, Little One, I was very lonely before you came. When I found the little baby goat near the edge of a meadow one rainy morning, I just couldn't leave her there. She had not been afraid of me when I touched her. And she was so weak that she could not stand up.

"She belonged to the only friend I ever had since I came to the mountain. Her name was Rachel." The big man smiled and looked at Jill. "I met Rachel when I made exchanges. She was very kind and often left fresh bread or cakes for me." Andrew's eyes were misty now as he remembered.

"I took the little kid to her that morning. She was already upset because she had found the mother dead the night before, but couldn't find the kid. We guessed the nanny died only hours after birth. Anyway, she could see how I already loved that baby and she asked me if I wanted to take her and try to raise her. She even supplied me with the fresh milk three times a week and I kept it chilled in that cold water in the milk can.

"So, I brought her here, and kept her inside the cave until the weather cleared up. I laid her on a hide beside the stove, and kept it burning so she would be warm. I fed her with a spoon...she was my friend for years," he said, as he stared at the snowy ground.

"I am *so* sorry Uncle Andrew! I know it must have hurt you a lot when she died," she said, leaning her head on his massive shoulder.

"Yes, Little one, because a few years ago, Rachel had died and I thought my heart would break. You see, I went one Wednesday afternoon to get milk and I was feeling really happy that day. I went toward the house and saw several cars and trucks parked outside. There were flowers on the door, and an old man was there...I knew he must have been her husband. He was crying." Andrew dabbed at his eyes with a cloth he clutched in his thick fingers. "I still put flowers on her grave sometimes."

Jill felt so much for the big, compassionate man. She grieved for his loneliness and the fact that his heart was so full of love and no one to share it with. She was glad she had made the decision to stay here with him like she had.

"Well, we're not going to let anything happen to your Ebony!" His exclamation startled Jill so that she jumped. He scrambled up from the log, unfolding his mighty frame, and went striding toward the horse. It was snowing harder now, but Andrew was oblivious to the crystals that caked his eyebrows and beard.

"We will build it right here! Make it about six feet high, and plenty big so he will have room to run around." He was very excited and was talking so fast, that Jill could scarcely understand him.

"What are you talking about, Uncle? What are you going to make?" She stood with her hands on her hips, smiling, relieved to see him happy again.

"A corral! We will build a corral for Ebony! What do you think of that, Little One?" He grabbed her around the waist and swung her high into the air.

"Ohhh," she squealed! "Uncle, you're nuts!" She laughed delightedly and he swung her again, twirling around and around. Suddenly, she went limp in his arms. He stopped all motion, not understanding what could be wrong with her.

"Little one? Baby?" He carried her like a baby into the cave. He was very frightened and gently laid her on the bed. There he knelt beside her, holding her hand between his thick strong hands. She looked so pale, and he was not sure if she was breathing.

Quickly, he went over to the milk can and wet a rag with the icy water. As he hurried back to the bedside, tears were streaming down his face, into his long, black beard, already wet with melted snow.

He began to wipe her face and then with relief, he saw the gentle rise and fall of her chest. Soon, she opened her eyes, trying to focus them.

"Wh… what happened? Wh… where am I?" Then she remembered. She could see how very scared Andrew was, and she smiled. "It's okay, I'm alright. Did I scare you, Uncle?"

Andrew was so relieved to see her smiling, that he laid his head on the bed and stifled a sob. Then he raised his head, looking at her through his misty eyes, he tried to laugh.

"You sure did, Little One," he said, as he gazed lovingly at her pale face. "What happened to you, anyway?"

She looked so frail, lying there with that sweet smile. "It's okay. I just fainted, I guess." She reached up and put her small hand on his wet beard. She knew it was time to tell him the truth.

Chapter 14

Susan, Mary, and their daughters squeezed into the cab of Bob's old blue pickup truck. They had wrapped some fruitcake and other Christmas treats to take to the Clarks.

Susan had left a note for Bob to call when he got in so that they could still be there when the Clarks got the news, whatever it might be. Old Jack and Randy decided to go back to Doc Jamison's and see how the little girl was doing. They wanted to see if there was anything they could do to help find the man responsible for ruining their Christmas, not to mention that little girl's!

As Old Jack and Randy tied their horses to Pete's wagon, in front of Doc's clinic, Jerry Davis came out. He had his head down, with his hat in his hands. It had begun to snow, and the snowflakes went down his collar, making him shiver. He put on his hat, and looked up at the sky, cursing the snow for coming now, when they needed to find the horse's tracks. Then he saw the two out by the wagon.

"How is the child? What's the news?" Old Jack asked as he raked his fingers through his tousled hair. He sensed by Jerry's somber expression that it could not be good.

***

Jerry's eyes were full of fear as he spoke. "Doc says she is in a coma. They are going to take her to the hospital over in Drayton. He did x-rays, and she has a severe skull injury. They don't know if she will ever regain consciousness," he stared at his booted foot as it made an arc in the snow. "It is just a terrible Christmas…"

His face was red with anger and he found himself visualizing the two torn bodies of the twins that terrible afternoon when he and the others had found them. His short legs pumped up and down as he continued.

"Are you coming with me over to the sheriff's? I want to help look for the monster that did this! With this snow, though, I doubt if we will be able to look for long." He paused, taking his hands from deep in his pants pockets.

"Oh, Jack, I think my brother will die if Bonnie doesn't come out of this!" Jerry was very near tears, as he tugged his warm hat down over his ears.

Jack nodded in agreement, put his hat back on, and handed Jerry's reins to him. "Yes, I know how you feel," he said soberly, "We're coming. Are you ready?"

Randy had taken it all in, still in a daze. He could not understand what was going on or why all these terrible things kept happening. He followed the two men in silence, fearful of what was to come. He wondered who would be next. When they got to the sheriff's office, no one was there, but they could see dozens of horse tracks in the snow, and started out immediately following them.

Within a few minutes, the trackers came into view. After a while, they all arrived at the site of the incident, and most of them were staying a few yards back, so that the sheriff and his deputy could check the area.

They found a man's boot tracks, and the horse's tracks. As far as they could tell, the man had not gotten on the horse, at least not near here, but had indeed followed the animal. They found a heavy club in the bloody snow and assumed that was what the man used to hit Bonnie.

Soon they were ready to begin. The snow was falling more heavily now, and they were pressed for time. The tracks led toward the river, still both sets in the same trail. By the time they got to the river, the snow was falling very heavily, and rapidly their own tracks began to fill behind them.

The river was frozen solidly along here, and they were not surprised when the tracks went right onto the river. The main problem here was that there were only very faint tracks for a hundred yards or more. The snow was constantly blown off the ice by the wind that whipped around the bend in the river there. What tracks they saw were barely visible here, so the men split up to see if they could find where the tracks left the river. They agreed to meet at this same spot in an hour to report. By then, it would be dark anyway. No one had much hope of finding anything now.

In an hour, they all returned and no one had found any tracks leaving the river. Deputy Bill Jackson had gone down the nearest roads and had not found any tracks, either.

"All I found was a car, stalled out past Widow Watson's meadow. I didn't recognize it, and it was abandoned. The hood was up, and I guess whoever it was walked into town. The snow had already covered any tracks. I took down the license number, anyway," Deputy Bill added formally.

"Well, who knows, maybe it belonged to the man who did this. We will go over there and wait for him to come back." The sheriff was relieved to have something concrete to do. After all, they had no other clues to go on.

They all rode the couple of miles to where the car had been parked. By then it was dark, and they were all cold and covered with the snow that fell continually. They looked like so many ghosts riding along. They neared the spot, and then got close enough to see that the car was gone! Even its tracks were gone, as if the car had never been there.

"Well, I'll be…" Deputy Bill was perplexed, pushing a finger under his hat to scratch his head. Right away, he went on the radio to report the license number. In a few moments, they received word that it was a stolen car.

"Well, that says a lot. We will put out a bulletin on it, and if the highway patrol finds it, then we've got him!"

***

Susan had taken Mary and Wilma Martin home, and she and June started for their cabin right away. Bob had called from the sheriff's office, and said he and Randy would meet them at home. The snow caused poor visibility, as she drove up toward the shed. It was joined to the well house, and they parked the pickup inside in bad weather. She was almost inside when she noticed everything was strewn all over the place. Boxes and garden tools and equipment of every kind was scattered everywhere. Near the door was a broken lantern.

"Mom, what has happened!? What's wrong?" June squealed.

Susan jerked the wheel, as she backed immediately out of the shed. "We're gonna wait by the bridge for your daddy. I don't know what is going on, but we're not staying around here to find out!"

A cold chill ran down her spine giving her an intense desire to scream. The events of this day were getting even more frightening.

They drove slowly down the road, unable to see but a few feet ahead because of the blinding snow. It was like a white wall shutting out the world and isolating them.

Susan was really afraid now, not knowing who or what had made the terrible mess in the shed. After the little girl had been attacked earlier, she thought anything might happen now.

"June, I want you to lock your door!" she commanded.

"I already did, Mom! I'm scared!" Silently, Susan locked hers, and reached over and took her daughter by the hand.

Soon the bridge came into view. She slowed the truck and was coming to a stop when she saw two riders on horseback crossing the bridge. She held her breath, praying it was Bob and Randy, but still fearful until she could make out their faces. Then, "Thank God, it's them!"

"Stay here!" She jumped out of the pickup and ran toward them. The snow clung to her eyelashes making it difficult to see, though the lights from the pickup illuminated the road for a few feet ahead. The snow was falling heavily now, each giant flake reflecting the light as it landed on Susan's dark hair.

"Bob! Bob, someone has been in the shed! I don't know if he went into the house or not. I left as soon as I saw the mess! What are we going to do?" She was clearly terrified and her fear made Bob cringe. Getting off the horse, and quickly putting his arms around her, he encouraged her with a tight hug.

"Now, settle down, Honey. I'll find out what is going on. Randy, you wait here with your mother and you all be praying. I'll be right back. If I don't come in fifteen minutes, go tell the sheriff."

With that, he hurried toward the cabin, although he allowed the horse to gingerly pick its way on the ice beneath the freshly fallen snow.

Susan stood for a moment and watched him disappear into a wall of white. Then, turning quickly, she and Randy climbed back into the truck. Susan forgot to lock her door again. She put her hands on the steering wheel and stared ahead in silence.

"Mom, is Daddy going back there? Why don't we go for the sheriff? June was beginning to cry. So many horrible things had happened, and it was just too much to bear. Randy sat in silence, his eyes wide with fear.

"Well, your daddy said for us to wait fifteen minutes, and if he isn't back, then we should go for Sheriff Billings. I'm so..! What if...?" She looked at her children, and seeing their young frightened faces, she reached across and pulled them into a hug. "We will just wait and see. Father God," she prayed, "keep Bob safe. Please don't let anything happen...please! In Jesus' name, amen."

She kept her eyes closed tightly, and still holding June's hand, began to repeat aloud, "Fear thou not; for I am with thee: be not dismayed; for I am thy God: I will strengthen thee; yea I will help thee; yea, I will uphold thee with the right hand of my righteousness."

The minutes dragged by, with Susan checking her watch every few seconds. Minute by minute she was becoming more and more anxious.

"I don't know if I can wait fifteen minutes," she said nervously.

The snow was quickly leaving a thick white blanket on the windshield, isolating them from the outside realities. It gave Susan no comfort though, as fear tried to take a firmer grip on her mind it made her heart pound. Yet the seconds ticked slowly by.

Suddenly, the door of the pickup opened and Susan was so startled that she screamed in terror and began to fight. With her eyes squeezed shut, she pounded on the unexpected intruder with her fists.

"Honey! Susan!! It's me, Bob!" He grasped her firmly by the wrists to stop her attack. The voice of her loved one was like music to Susan's ears as she realized who it was. She was so relieved that she began crying hysterically and June and Randy were crying and laughing at the same time.

"Mama, it's alright! It's Daddy! Oh, Daddy, you scared us half to death!" June reached across Randy to her mother, patting her shoulder reassuringly as he awkwardly patted his mother's knee.

Taking Susan in his arms and holding her trembling body next to his, he said, "Well, are you okay, Honey? I didn't mean to scare you. In fact, you scared me pretty bad, too," he laughed shakily. Looking across at his children, he said with an encouraging smile, "There is no one at the cabin, or on the place. Everything is okay and the only thing I couldn't find was the extra five gallons of gas." Bob had already decided that the man who had run out of gas on the road had stolen their gas. What he did not understand was why the man would hit a small child and take her horse.

Chapter 15

There were only a few soft rays of light in the cave. Jill knew it must be very early in the morning. She snuggled down into her covers, and lay there watching the giant of a man on the pallet across the room. He made an enormous mountain, she thought, with all those blankets and animal hides over his big frame. He slept peacefully, snoring very softly every once in a while.

Jill remembered last night and how wonderful he had been. She had told him the whole truth, including the secret she had held in her heart for so long. She was contented now, with everything out in the open. She knew he would take care of her for as long as necessary.

She thought of Larry now, as she had so many mornings and nights. She felt like she had betrayed him and did not know how she would ever live without him. The thought made her heart break, but she knew she would never go back to Madison. After all, everyone thought she was dead, and she was convinced that the best thing to do would be to just let them believe that. She missed them so much, but she knew her parents had accepted her death already. And Larry? As she prayed for him, the tears welled up in her eyes. "Please, Lord," she whispered determinedly, "help him find someone else and have a full and wonderful life."

She could remember the picture of her parents in the newspaper. It broke her heart to see them in so much pain. It was taken at the scene of her disappearance a few weeks later. They had all given her up for dead, and the entire community had come out to the beautiful woods that fall day. They had a precious memorial service, there in the cool breeze, with the amber leaves falling all around them.

Jill had saved the article and picture, as she had all the others before the service. Uncle Andrew always got newspapers on the day he "made exchanges". He had done this for years and had saved every paper. There were stacks and stacks of papers in the back of the cave. Jill had enjoyed looking at those old papers, some of them so old and brittle that they tried to fall apart in her hands.

As she turned over on her back, she remembered that awful day when she came across the big story about the twins' disappearance. Her best friend, Wilma, had been crushed when she lost her brothers. It was odd, because Uncle Andrew had told her he had seen the twins the same day everyone was looking for them, but he had not known about the search. The man with them was playing some kind of game with the boys. They had blindfolds over their eyes, and sat real still while the man hid something in the trees.

Jill had been horrified, when Uncle Andrew told her this, because she was not sure at all that the man had been playing a game. When she asked him about it, he agreed, saying that when he had thought about it later, he had gone back but no one was there. All he found were the red bandannas and he had put them in his pocket. He told her that he lost them the same night he had found her in the woods.

It was not until two weeks later when he saw in the paper that they were dead, that he realized the possibility of foul play.

Because of his shyness, he would not go to the town, not wanting to reveal himself or maybe even be accused. He had not had a good look at the man anyway, he had told her.

Jill did not like to think about the twins and had never mentioned them except the one time they talked about the story in the newspaper. Andrew had not realized she knew the boys.

She smiled, thinking how wonderful it would be now, to talk about her family and Larry, and all that had meant so very much to her. Uncle Andrew had sat quietly on the side of Jill's bed last night, when she told him she could remember her past. He was so happy, thinking that her memory had come back. He had bent over and kissed her on the forehead and big tears came into his eyes. "Thank God," he had said.

"But, Uncle Andrew," she had told him, swallowing hard, "I never really lost my memory. I have lied to you! But, I promise I will *never* lie to you again! I just had to have a place to stay and I was afraid you would make me go back home if you knew the truth. I'm so very sorry." She had looked away, blinking back stubborn tears, not able to look into his eyes.

He gently took her face in his hands and turned it so he could look into her eyes. "Little One, I would never make you go back if you didn't want to. I'm happy that you wanted to stay here with *me*, anyway. I never thought I could be as happy with another person as I have been with you. I thought that being alone was the only way I could live. I love you, Little One, and to me you are my child. No matter where you are, or what you do, I will always remember how you filled my life."

Jill laid there, her eyes brimming with tears at the memory of the kind man's words. Now, I can bear anything, she thought. She remembered his compassion as she had quietly and solemnly told him of her terminal illness. She told him how the doctor had done some more blood tests, but it was evident that she had leukemia. She knew they would do all they could to prolong her life, but she knew eventually the leukemia would kill her. She had told Andrew of seeing her

105

parents weeping the night before the hayride and how it would have been so difficult for them to see her suffer for months and months. She had cried and cried as Andrew held her in his arms.

She had not told Larry about her diagnosis, and now that she knew he thought her to be dead already, she was glad she had not told him. She thanked God that he and her family did not have to watch her slowly die.

And now, with Uncle Andrew to take care of her and love her, she could quietly live out her life and look forward to going home to be with Jesus. She smiled as she remembered sharing her Lord Jesus with Uncle Andrew and his child-like joy as they knelt together there in the little cave.

He prayed, asking forgiveness from God, expressing his belief that Jesus is the Son of God and that He died for his sins and rose again, and is sitting at the right hand of the Father.

Andrew had been overjoyed as Jill explained so many things to him that he had wondered about for years. They shared the peace of God when she told of Jesus' words that He would never leave them or forsake them.

Jill felt tears trickle down the sides of her face as she lay on her back remembering last night. Now, she and Uncle Andrew had the most lasting bond of all and she knew that the angels in heaven were rejoicing because he had become a true child of God. She also knew that through the power of the Lord they would be strong until the very end.

She could hear him beginning to stir, and she stretched, feeling all was well with her new life. He looked over at her, peeking out from under his pile of covers.

"Mornin', Little One," he smiled.

106

"Mornin', Uncle Andy," she said with a grin.

He thought about that for a few minutes, and then, sitting up, he said, "Little One, you have never called me Uncle *Andy* before! And I like it! I guess I should call you Jill now, huh? It will be strange for a while, but I guess I will get used to it! Uncle Andy? Huh…" he mused.

Looking at her, he smiled a heartwarming smile and headed for the stove. Jill stretched again, and all was well with her. She could not know what horrors and fears were coming their way in the near future.

Chapter 16

Bob had called Sheriff Billings after getting his family safely back into the cabin. The snow had drifted around the door that evening. In his haste to check for an intruder, Bob had tracked a lot of it onto the floor so that when the family returned, it was wet. Susan and June were busy cleaning up the mess while Bob talked on the phone.

"Mama, why do you think someone would steal gas like that? We would have given him some if he had only asked," June said flatly.

"I know, Honey. I guess he must have been in a big hurry or something." She turned as Bob hung up the telephone.

"Bob, did I hear you say something about someone running out of gas?" Susan asked him as she wiped up the last of the melted snow.

"Yeah, Deputy Bill found a car on the road that was empty and the hood was up. When we all went back later to check on it, there was not a trace. Bill had taken the license number and found out it was stolen. We had guessed that it was out of gas, and since our gas is missing, I'm sure of it now. Billings said he thought it just might have been the same man who hit little Bonnie. I guess he wanted her horse pretty bad, huh?"

"What if he comes back, Daddy? I'm scared!" June stood up from where she was still kneeling there on the floor. "Daddy, where's Husky?"

Bob and Susan exchanged uneasy glances. Bob had told her that he had missed the dog when he had come back to check the house. He had called and called, but could not find him anywhere. As he had checked the yard and garden area with a flashlight, he had looked for the dog's tracks and those of the intruder. None could be found in the heavy snow cover which deepened every minute in the storm.

***

In the early morning light, Bob went out into the clear, still air. His breath hung in icy crystals before slowly falling into oblivion. He wondered how on earth all these gruesome, mysterious things could be happening in such a beautiful place as this. The snow had fallen much of the night and had left a silken blanket over the earth. There was no trace of the events of the previous night. Not even a track remained to show that they had all come into the house long after dark.

"Husky?" Bob called quietly. "Come on, big fella…come on!"

What could have happened to him, Bob wondered. He stepped from the wooden porch into the sunshine, shading his eyes from the glare. He sunk in the snow nearly to his knees. He thought of another time, a carefree time, when, as a boy he had stepped into deep snow and stood there, pretending he was on another planet. He remembered the wonderful sensation of falling backward into the soft cushion of snow. After making several imprints of his own body, he would pretend each imprint was a Martian. His lips curved up into a small smile as the memories flitted through his mind. As Bob struggled through the deep snow, he longed for the simple happy days when things were right in his world.

He went to the barn where the horses were snug and dry. After they were fed and the ice on their water had been broken, Bob started back to the cabin, ready and thankful for the cup of steaming coffee he knew his wife would have waiting.

109

He stopped with one foot in the air, poised for another step. He listened, turning his head from side to side. I guess I'm hearing things, he thought, and started through the snow again.

"Nooo," There it was again, he thought. He could not believe he was hearing that frightened muffled cry.

"Husky? Husky? Where are you?" Bob called into the morning air.

He had heard that cry before, many years ago. He had taken his little family to the country for a respite from their hectic city life. They were visiting Susan's grandparents on their dairy farm. The children always loved going there to see all the animals. They seemed especially drawn to Porkie, Grandpa's cattle dog.

She was a brilliant animal, responding to any command and working harder that any dog would be expected to. Porkie loved June and Randy, too, and her bright eyes flashed that day as they came into the barn.

There she was in a wooden stall on a pile of clean hay. Beside her were eight adorable pups sucking greedily. Each was different in his own way and only one was identical to his mother. This pup was whining softly, having been pushed away by his larger, stronger brothers and sisters. He was the ninth pup, the "runt of the litter".

"Oh, Daddy, look at this one! He's hungry! Hey, you guys move over and let him eat!" Randy gently moved a couple of the pups away and placed the small warm body at his mother's side.

The boy sat back on his heels, satisfied with his good deed. Then the sensitive five-year-old was dismayed to see the others immediately shove the pup aside. Randy picked it up and held him close. While he sat there letting the puppy suck on his little finger he became aware of his father and grandpa talking quietly.

"Yep, it's too bad about the little runt. He's awfully weak and there just isn't room for him to nurse. I guess I'll have to take him out this afternoon and put him out of his misery," the old gentleman said with genuine sadness. "He will starve otherwise," he said with a shrug, shaking his head, and shoving his weathered hands into the pockets of his overalls.

"Grandpa!" June shrieked, jumping up from beside Porkie. "You can't do that! He's so sweet, and besides, he looks just like Porkie!"

Randy rushed to Bob, pulling at his sleeve with his free hand. "Daddy, can we take him home, can we? We could feed him with a bottle! He wouldn't be any trouble, I promise!"

"Please, Daddy? Grandpa? Can we, please? We don't want him to die!"

June had tears shining in her eyes and stood looking up at her father with her hand over her brother's as they protected the tiny living creature.

The two men looked at each other, mutual doubt spreading over their faces. "Honey, he is going to die. He's too weak and he's only three days old," their Grandpa said gently.

"But, can't we try?" June's tears were flowing freely now, as were Randy's.

He said, "Daddy, if I was weak when I was little, would you try to help me?" His little chin quivered as he cupped his hands around the tiny baby. Still the pup sucked Randy's finger.

"Randy," Bob started to respond to his son, but was interrupted. "Grandpa, if he could only get milk from my finger he would be okay," he said, sadly resigned now to the fate of his little friend.

Bob turned to the old man, "Grandpa, what do you think? Would he have a chance at home?"

111

The two youngsters' faces brightened hopefully as they looked from Bob toward the old man for the answer they truly wanted to hear.

"Well, he does seem to have enough strength to suck. He's a husky little fella to be so small," Grandpa thoughtfully pulled on his ear as the silent group looked to him for wisdom and guidance.

An eternity of seconds went by while he took the pup and carefully examined his lips and gums. "Well…" He looked from June to Randy to Bob, who even appeared hopeful at that point. "You would have to feed him diluted milk and raw eggs at least every two hours as first," he said, a frown creasing his forehead.

With a grin, Bob said to his children, "We could do that, couldn't we?"

"Oh yesss, Daddy!" they shrieked. "Thank you, Grandpa, thank you!" They grasped each other by the hands and began laughing and dancing in a circle, jumping up and down.

"Hold on there, now," Grandpa said firmly. "This is serious business, you know. And he still might not make it."

Bob remembered how he had taken the tiny black puppy into his hands and said, "You *will* make it! You're a husky fella, aren't you?" He had looked at the children and said, "That's what we will call him! Husky!"

Again, the quiet cry, whining, seeming even weaker and more far away than before. Bob followed the muffled sound, or at least tried to go toward it. He called softly, listening intently for his canine friend's pitiful reply. Going this way, it would get weaker, the other way, where he just knew he was, Bob could not find anything.

By the time Bob had located the animal, he had made dozens and dozens of tracks in the snow near the barn and frozen creek. The dog had crawled into a slight depression near the creek and the snow had completely covered the hiding place. As soon as Bob realized the dog was there, he fell to his knees, calling softly. "Husky, I'm here. It's alright, fella. Husky? Husky?"

Soon he could feel the furry body as he frantically scraped the snow away with his gloved hands, wiping it gently from his black eyes. Husky no longer made any noise, but looked into Bob's face as he raised the animal's head. With a gasp, Bob saw that the dog had been struck on the back of the neck where a deep gash was clotted over with blood and snow.

"Poor fella... what on earth happened to you? It's a wonder you didn't freeze to death out here." He cooed gently to the pet as he carefully examined him for other injuries. Then he gently lifted Husky out of his bed of snow and started for the cabin.

As he trudged through the deep snow, he remembered how they had carried him into Grandpa's house years ago and had given him his first warm milk and egg formula. Grandma had found an old eye dropper and Husky had eaten greedily until his little sides poked out.

After they took him home, he gained strength every day and the whole family helped with his feedings. Susan said it was just like having a baby in the house and grew fonder of him as each day passed. They took him back to visit the farm when he was about two months old. Bob remembered now, the special celebration they had had in the old farm kitchen, in honor of his survival.

Bob looked down at the limp body in his arms, ninety-five pounds of runt. His eyes filled with tears as he wondered if their Husky would survive this time. He fervently prayed that he would.

Chapter 17

The day after Christmas, the story was in the newspapers in Madison and Drayton. "Child Attacked by Unknown Assailant in Madison" read the impersonal headline.

Jill was stunned as she read the story a few days later. Andy had brought several papers in that morning, and she was spending a relaxing, warm afternoon reading and drinking hot tea.

She sat up on the side of the bed where she had been lying and her heart began beating faster as she read the details.

"The child's horse was chased away and she was left for dead. She was able to tell her uncle that a large man had struck her and taken her horse. The animal was a young black male with a black and silver saddle. If any person has information leading to the recovery of the horse and/or identity of the assailant, please contact the newspaper, or the police departments in Madison or Drayton."

Jill slowly and deliberately folded the newspaper to the article and laid it on her lap. She sat there smoothing it absently as her mind raced. She thought about the beautiful black pony tied out there in the new corral that Uncle Andy had not even finished. He did fit the description exactly and Uncle Andy did bring him home the same day that the little girl was hurt.

No, it just couldn't be, she thought to herself, shaking her head. It just simply could not be possible.

She did not know how long she had been sitting there. Finally, she laid the paper carefully under her blankets until she could decide what to do. Evening was coming on, and she went to the wood stove and carefully built up the fire.

Mechanically, she prepared to fry the rabbit Uncle Andy had brought in a couple of days ago. He had had it soaking in cold water to tenderize it. She could remember how impressed she had first been with the change of the reddish colored meat after soaking. It became light pink, much like the meat of a chicken. After cooking, it tasted delicious. She thought about the many things Uncle Andy had taught her since she had been with him.

A tear rolled down her cheek and she just knew he would never hurt anyone. He had always been so kind and gentle with her. He was a very generous person, and she felt like if he ever could overcome his tremendous shyness, he would be loved by all who would get to know him. No, she thought! "He couldn't have done this terrible thing! There has to be an explanation, there just has to be…" she said aloud to the empty cave.

Soon the meal was prepared and she sat everything on the back of the stove to keep it warm. She had made a pot of coffee and sat now with a big steaming mug at the tree trunk table. She had gotten the other papers off her bed and had folded each to the daily articles telling of little Bonnie's condition. They were stacked in front of her and she read each one in succession, hoping against hope that the child had recovered. It was not to be, at least not yet.

Bonnie still laid in a coma in the hospital in Drayton and there had been no reports of the missing horse or the big man who had attacked her. A week had passed since the incident. It was New Year's Day.

Jill remembered how she and Uncle Andy had stayed up last night to see in the New Year. He said it had been the first time he had done this since he had been on the mountain. She taught him "Auld Lang

115

Syne", and they had said a prayer for the safety and good health of her family and Larry.

She got up to refill her cup. Stepping to the stove, she saw that it was fully dark outside. Still Uncle Andy had not returned home. She walked to the entrance of the cave, carrying the steaming black coffee with her. She looked toward the corral where the moonlight made Ebony's black head look like a silhouette and she had once made on black paper in school.

"Where are you, Uncle Andy?" she said with a shiver. Outside there was a snow muffled silence in the clear moonlit night.

***

It was dark and cold. There was a musty sweet smell of apples and onions in the air. The big man tried to lift himself but the throbbing in his head kept him immobile. He tried to focus his eyes but he could not see anything. He wondered vaguely if he was blind. His cheek rested against the damp, cold earth. He could hear something dripping somewhere, and he thought he heard the squeak of a mouse.

His right knee was bent and the left foot was elevated. He tried to turn on his back but something was behind him and he could not roll over. He had a deep need to turn over, but his head throbbed so terribly that he was unable to. He did manage to draw up his left knee and when he did, his foot slid off something hard. He began to move his mouth, trying to find some moisture there. He desperately wanted a drink of water. He slept.

Chapter 18

Husky was lying beside the wood stove in the kitchen. He was resting after a tiring early morning walk through the house. His recuperation was very slow, but the worst seemed to be over.

Susan was cooking breakfast and glanced over at him. "Did those kids wear you out, fella? You have to take it easy, you know. After all, we nearly lost you and you need to take it slow for a while."

Husky did not raise his head, but his ears turned back as he listened to the soft sound of her voice. His eyes followed her movements around the kitchen and he wagged his tail when she came close to him. Twice, he whined softly, and she reached down and patted him on the head.

As she slowly stirred the fresh milk gravy, she remembered how she had felt when Bob had come into their cabin carrying the great animal in his arms. Even now, a lump came in her throat as she recalled the tears of anguish on her husband's face that morning. She and the children had all thought the dog to be dead. He was completely limp…even his active tail drooped, and the gash on the back of his head was grotesquely opened.

"Bob?" she had gasped, rushing to them. They had fallen to their knees with the dog between them. The children heard their mother's distressed voice and came from their bedrooms where they had been dressing for breakfast.

"Where did you find him, Daddy? Is he…is he dead? The children had been terribly upset that morning, and they stayed close as their parents dressed the wound and carefully dried the dog's wet fur. June and Susan prepared a bed beside the woodstove and placed a bowl of water nearby. Bob carried Husky into the kitchen and gently placed him on the rugs, covering him with an old coat.

They watched over him all that day, waiting for him to wake up. Occasionally, one of them would bathe his muzzle with a warm wet rag. Late in the day, he began licking the rag, but did not appear to be awake. They offered the water to him, even to the point of opening his mouth and gently pouring a little water from a spoon between his jaws.

Susan could remember their getting up during the night that first night and checking on him. It had been well after midnight when Bob had awakened her. She struggled out of a deep disturbing dream to him shaking her shoulder and calling her name.

"Susan, Susan! Wake up! I think Husky will be alright! He was awake for a few minutes and even wagged his tail!" She came fully awake and went quickly with him to the kitchen, as she pulled on her robe.

"He seems to be sleeping more restfully, doesn't he?" Bob said, with his arm across his wife's hair where it laid tumbling down her back.

Susan smiled now, still very relieved to see those bright eyes looking up at her as she crooned. "I sure wish you could talk, big fella. I know you would have a tale to tell, wouldn't you?"

Now it was the day after New Year's Day, over a week since that awful Christmas afternoon, and they still had not found that stolen car. And, Susan was thinking, poor little Bonnie might never wake up to tell us what happened that day.

A sudden commotion from the living room startled her. "Mom! Mom! Come quick! Hurry!" Randy was excitedly jumping from one foot to the other, rushing toward the kitchen, then back to the front door of the cabin. "Hurry! It's Widow Watson…she's hurt bad!"

118

Susan quickly took the pan of gravy off the stove and grabbed a wet towel. Rushing out the door, she was aghast to see poor Mrs. Watson on her knees out by the creek. There was blood in her hair and the old woman held her hands over her face. Her shoulders were shaking with hard, deep sobs. She knelt in the deep snow, unaware of her bare knees above her knee boots. She was shivering violently.

"Mrs. Watson?" Susan gently put her hand on the disheveled woman's shoulder. The old woman shrieked and turned toward Susan. Her pitiful battered face made tears spring instantly to Susan's eyes.

Recognition flashed across Widow Watson's face, and she frantically clutched Susan's hand. "Oh, thank God I found someone! It's Marie Jamison! He was after her!" She held her face in her hands, trying to control her sobbing.

"Mrs. Watson, calm down. It will be alright. Why don't you come on into the cabin where it is warm? You need a doctor." Susan was horrified that someone had hurt this poor old lady.

"Doctor? Doctor! Oh Dear God in heaven! It's Marie, Doc's mother! We have to go help her!" The large woman struggled to her feet and tried to pull Susan back towards the woods.

"Please, Mrs. Watson. We have to get help and take care of you. You are…" Susan caught the woman around the waist as she fainted.

"Randy! Call your daddy from the barn! Hurry!" She stood there, struggling to support the woman who was forty pounds heavier than she. Randy rushed away, swinging his arms as he fought his way through the deep snow.

Within a moment, Bob came running. He picked up the old woman easily with a questioning glance at

Susan. Heading for the cabin, he turned to her. "What on earth has happened?"

"I'm not sure, Honey. Randy found her out here by the creek. She was crying something about Marie Jamison being hurt."

"Well, you better go call the Doc and see if he can come right away. I wonder what happened to his mother."

They both went into the cabin and Bob gently laid Mrs. Watson on the couch. June had been out exercising one of the horses and came in moments later. As she bathed Mrs. Watson's face with a cool wet cloth, Bob elevated her feet.

"Oh, look at her poor knees," Bob said. They were both bright red and the dreaded white patches of frostbite were beginning. Her knees were bruised and skinned from falling. June carefully wiped them after squeezing the rag out in fresh water. Her face and hands were partially frostbitten as well. It appeared that she had been out all night long.

"Here's a blanket, Daddy," Randy came into the room with a warm comforter and helped Bob and June cover up their patient.

Susan hung the phone up and turned to Bob. Her face was white and there were tears in her eyes. "Bob," she began, "Doc's coming right over. And Bob, his mother is not there. He said she went over to Widow Watson's yesterday to spend a couple of days. What could have happened this time?" Her voice and her face were filled with anguish.

She put her knuckles against her mouth and tears made silent tracks down her face. Silently she backed up to the fireplace, looking very young and frightened.

"Mama? Are you alright?" June moved to her side and put an arm around her mother. Susan nodded, not

120

taking her hand from her mouth. Widow Watson began to moan and cry again. She was trying to get up from the couch and Bob gently held her back. Susan stepped up and stood behind him with her hand on his shoulder. She quoted aloud Isaiah 41:10.

"Fear thou not; for I am with thee: be not dismayed; for I am thy God: I will strengthen thee; yea, I will help thee; yea, I will uphold thee with the right hand of my righteousness."

"Mrs. Watson, you rest easy. The Doctor will be here any minute. We are going to find Mrs. Jamison. Don't you worry now," Bob already had his jacket on and had called the sheriff. They were going to meet some other men at the Widow Watson's. He knew they needed to know more, so he pulled a stool up beside Mrs. Watson. Taking her gently by the hand, he asked her what had happened.

***

"Well, we went for a walk before supper. We stayed on the trail because the snow was so deep," Mrs. Watson closed her eyes as it all came back to her.

It had been a clear evening, and they were enjoying the sparkling snowy forest. Tiny ice crystals fell from towering trees and reflected the light from the setting sun, as they shimmered to the blanket of snow on the forest floor. The ladies had been walking near the river for less than an hour. They talked quietly, enjoying the fresh air and the company of a good friend.

They had seen animal tracks in the snow on the frozen river. After a time, they noticed the tracks of a man coming onto the path. They followed them along, vaguely curious. Soon the tracks left the path and the two women looked at one another and into the woods in the direction the tracks led.

Not far into the trees, they could see a man in a green army jacket bending over something. He had a shovel and was carefully digging in the frozen ground. He had what appeared to be a crowbar, and would hack at the soil and then scoop the black earth up and place it in a neat pile. The forest was silent except for the digging sounds the stranger made and the sound of his breathing, rasping as if he were desperate for air.

"What do you think he is doing?" Marie whispered to Mrs. Watson.

"I don't know, but I don't think we should bother him, do you?" Mrs. Watson waved her hand as if they ought to leave, but Marie said in a very low voice, "No, let's wait until he's done and see who it is."

They were unaware that he had seen them. He had decided to refill the hole and then quickly and fearfully began to cover it with snow. He turned around and stopped as he saw that they continued to watch. The three stood in stony silence. The man's face was scarred from burns and his tousled black hair and wild eyes made him appear fearsome. His forehead glistened with perspiration.

His black mustache hung grotesquely as it mingled with his scrubby beard. It appeared that the big man's beard was an attempt to hide the horrible scars, but it only served to accentuate them. His breath came in short, quick clouds of fog.

"Hello? Are you lost? Can we help you with something?" Marie said kindly.

His appearance seemed not to affect her at all and she never blinked an eye. Widow Watson looked at her, unsure about speaking to this horrid stranger.

"Marie," she whispered urgently.

"Marie, we'd better be getting on back home, don't you think?" Mrs. Watson was wishing they had turned back the minute they had seen the man's tracks. She tugged urgently at her friend's arm.

"It's alright, Watson," Marie said reassuringly. She had always called her that. It was a game they had played when they were both young married women. Their husbands had been boyhood friends, and the two couples had spent many hours together, living, growing, and learning. Later on, the two women shared the deaths of their husbands…first Marie's, and four years later, Mrs. Watson's. They had been separated only by distance and had remained close friends for many, many years.

"What are you two doing here?" The big man talked quietly through clenched teeth. "How long have you been standing there?"

"Oh, not long, Mister. We were just going home," Widow Watson was indeed ready to leave, but Marie's curiosity got the better of her.

"What were you doing back there?" she asked with a bright look on her face.

Mrs. Watson thought how she hated Marie's insatiable curiosity at times like this. Even when they were young, she would always go that extra step it took them to get into trouble.

"Marie! Don't bother the man with a lot of questions! Now come on, we *have* to be going!" Mrs. Watson stepped away from Marie, not caring that she was headed in the wrong direction. The man made her feel so uneasy, and she was just ready to be anywhere but there.

As the two women discussed what they would do, the man was coming closer and closer to them. Suddenly Mrs. Watson saw him raise his arm and she screamed, "Nooooo…!"

The man had struck at her friend but as he heard the scream, he turned on his heel so that the blow only grazed Marie's shoulder. He took the handle of the shovel and slammed it into Mrs. Watson's soft stomach. A puff of air came from her mouth as she bent double. She felt a fist come up from below her face and strike her full across the jaw. She fell to the ground gasping, "Run, Marie! Run!"

Then she lay still, horrified and half conscious. Suddenly, there was a hard blow struck against the side of her head as the man hit her with the scoop of the shovel.

Leaving her for dead, he went after Marie, who was fleeing as rapidly as possible through the snow on the path.

***

Mrs. Watson looked into Bob's face now, through her tears of anguish. "Oh, Dear God," she wept. "I just know he has killed her. Why, oh why did he want to hurt us?" Deep sobs shook her body as she pushed her fists into her eyes.

Bob could feel anger rising in the depths of his stomach but he said slowly and carefully, "Mrs. Watson, can you remember where you were when you saw this man?"

"Oh, it was at least a mile past the bridge on my side of the river," Mrs. Watson sniffed and wiped her eyes. "But Marie was running toward my house when I last saw her. I must have fainted because when I woke up, it was dark. I couldn't hear anything… just awful silence." The distraught old woman began to cry again and held her head with her hands.

"Ooh, my head hurts so bad," she said softly.

"Can you tell us what the man looked like? Just one more time?" Bob said as the sheriff came through the door. The doctor had been standing there for several dreadful moments, his lips pressed together in a grim line, his hands fisted at his sides.

124

"He was a large man in a green army jacket… he had messy black hair and a nasty black beard. His face was scarred something awful, he was horrible." She spoke slowly and painfully, as it was a strain to remember.

"Oh, Marieeee," she sobbed. "Please go find Marie!!!" she said as she closed her eyes. The tears squeezed out and ran down the sides of her face.

Bob put his arm around Doc Jamison's shoulder as the group went toward the door. Patting his friend awkwardly, he tried to reassure the frightened man.

"We'll find her, Doc," he said, knowing full well that they might find something they did not want to find.

Chapter 19

It was before daylight and already Jill was dressed and ready to go look for Uncle Andy. She had spent a long sleepless night worrying about the story in the newspaper and Andy's possible involvement. She could not imagine where he would be all night long… he was usually never later than sunset.

Supper still sat on the back of the stove, untouched. She had lost what little appetite she had while waiting for him to come home. Now she took a piece of the fried rabbit and poured herself another cup of hot black coffee from the pot she had kept ready all night. She had hoped he would come in, probably cold and hungry, and she wanted to have everything ready. She knew they had to talk.

As she moved about the cave, she ate the meat and sipped the hot coffee, wincing at the strong bitter taste. She pulled her hair back into a pony tail and tucked it under the warm cap Uncle Andy had brought for her only a few weeks ago. As she reached for the bridle, the small statue she had carved of him caught her eye. She picked it up and tears came into her eyes at the memory of that Christmas Day and his tenderness. I pray that he is not hurt somewhere, she thought. Absently, she put the small carving into her coat pocket. After pulling on her gloves, she carried the saddle outside toward the half-finished corral.

Moments later, she was riding Ebony through the forest in the early morning twilight. She knew the sun would be up soon, and she would be able to see more clearly.

Thank God it did not snow last night, she thought. At least I can follow his tracks. I just hope no one sees me. I couldn't bear that. She brushed a wisp of hair from her face and took a long deep breath of the cold morning air.

She followed the tracks as they lead from one homestead to another, ever a visible trail. It was mid-morning as she topped the hill above Widow Watson's place. The scene below confused and frightened her. A police car was there, and the ambulance lights were flashing. There were several people scurrying around, and two men were carefully placing someone on a stretcher. Jill gasped and threw her gloved hand to her mouth as one of the men gently pulled a sheet over the face of the body. "Not Widow Watson!" Her heart cried in anguish, as she whispered the awful words.

Jill looked down beside where she and the horse stood and gloomily saw that the tracks she had been following definitely led on down the hill… right for the Widow's place. She shaded her eyes and looked searchingly at each of the men who were moving around down there. No…Uncle Andy was not there. There was no one in the police car.

Suddenly, from out of the trees near the barn, two men came running. They were shouting and pointing in the direction they had come. One of them bent and grasped his knees as if he were trying to catch his breath. When he rose up, Jill saw that it was Larry… "Oh, Larry!" she gasped and wheeled her horse around. "I *can't* think about him anymore," she told herself. "I have to find Uncle Andy!"

She made a wide circle around to the area where the men had been pointing. Before long, she came to the path Uncle Andy had taken. Here the other men's tracks stopped as they obviously figured they could not overtake this strong runner on foot. They had made numerous tracks of their own as they stamped around in dismay and disgust before turning back to the Watson place.

127

Jill immediately wheeled her horse, spurring him to gallop through the deep snow. Uncle Andy had chosen an overgrown path and soon Jill had to let the horse walk, picking his way through the brush.

Snow laden branches slapped her in the face more than once, and she kept her face down as much as possible, looking up only enough to make sure they still followed Andy's trail.

She felt chilled as she rode, and she placed her free hand in the deep, warm pocket of her coat. Bumping something hard, she pulled it out with a puzzled look on her face. "How did…?" And then she remembered putting it there as she prepared to leave the cave that morning.

At that moment, the horse stopped, making a whinnying sound. He stepped back, and Jill looked ahead of him.

Her heart came up in her throat as she wondered what had frightened him. She pulled the reins to make Ebony step back more. She looked again, not understanding what she was seeing there.

She looked behind her. Yes, there were Uncle Andy's tracks trampled beneath those of her horse, and they did lead up to this very spot. And across the way, she could see them leading into the snowy forest.

Here the snow had been disturbed, as if someone had been digging recently. It appeared that Andy had stopped to see what had occurred here. Or perhaps he had buried something here, Jill thought.

Knowing she had no time to waste, she hesitated only a moment and hastily moved to put the statue back in her pocket. She was clumsy with her gloves on and was unaware that it fell in the snow, as she urged the horse across the disturbed piece of ground and into the snowy woods.

She knew this area well, and from what Uncle Andy had told her many weeks ago she was sure he had been here before. Now his tracks led onto the path near the river. Jill stopped the horse and saw that there were other tracks here. Two sets, as if two people had been walking side by side.

She wondered vaguely if Uncle Andy had talked to someone on this path today. She rode easier now, with a clear trail to follow and watched ahead of her mechanically, knowing Uncle Andy would be far ahead by now because she had to go so slow in the woods.

When she saw the crimson strain on the snow, she caught her breath, "Blood!?" She whispered, as she frantically looked all around. There were numerous tracks there, three or four sets at least, she thought. One set led off the path toward the river, but they were not Uncle Andy's, so she went on, fearing that he had come to some kind of harm.

"Wait! Hold on there!" A man was shouting behind Jill. She turned sideways in the saddle to look back and was dismayed to see several men hurrying her way.

Immediately, she spurred the horse and pulling her warm cap down low, leaned forward, and urged him to run. Oh, please, God, don't let them recognize me! She looked straight ahead and went far out of her way before making her way to the cave. Somehow she knew Uncle Andy would be there.

***

"Well, I wonder who that was." Sheriff Billings scratched his head.

"I don't know, but I think I know that horse!" Jerry Davis said, hitching up his pants. With them were Larry Miller and Bob Greyson.

"You don't mean…?" Bob put his hand on Jerry's shoulder. "Was that little Bonnie's horse?" he asked, looking toward the path where the horse and rider had disappeared into the forest.

"Yes, Bob. I'm nearly positive. I couldn't see the saddle well, but I'm pretty sure," Jerry said, his red face twitching with excitement.

The sheriff turned to the men and said, "Those horses ought to be here pretty soon, don't you think? Come on, let's look over this area and see if we can figure out what happened. When we get those horses, we will follow the tracks that big man left over at the Widow's." The men nodded their agreement as he continued, "Jerry, you and Larry go on down the path a ways and see where these tracks go and Bob will go with me into the trees here and see if we can find out what this stranger was doing in there."

It was beginning to cloud up as the two went into the woods. Bob looked up through the barren trees and mentioned the fact that snow had been in the weather forecast the night before.

"I know it," said Sheriff Billings with disgust. He kicked at a low bush in frustration. "The weather has definitely not been on our side, has it? Say, what's this?" He hurried his steps to the mess in the snow. He held up a crowbar that had been partially covered with snow tossed by the horse's hooves. It had dirt on the end and a dark stain toward the middle.

"It looks like someone was digging here," Bob said. He was on his knees pushing the dirt and snow away. He looked up absently and started, seeing the crowbar he had missed only yesterday.

"Good grief, that's my crowbar! How'd it get here?" Bob reached up and took it. He leaned back on his heels and carefully examined it. He nodded his head,

130

repeating, "It's mine, alright. See my mark here? I put that on all my hand tools and axes and things." He looked up at Sheriff Billings, "It must have been taken the same night as my gas was stolen, huh?"

"Well," the lawman said, "let's see what that big fella buried here. I'll put the crowbar over here until we get ready to go. Maybe we will find some prints on it." He turned and stooped to lay the tool down when he saw a small dark object in the snow.

"Bob," he said with a peculiar sound in his voice, "look at this!" Incredulously, he handed the small brown statue to Bob. It was a husky looking man with bushy hair and a beard. He had no shirt or shoes, but otherwise fit the description of the stranger exactly.

They knew, because they had seen the man back at Widow Watson's place. The men had met at her house to begin a search for Marie Jamison. Sheriff Billings and Bob had driven up in the police car just as one other car arrived. Bob had immediately gotten out of the car as the sheriff called in to the police station.

"Sheriff, look!!" Bob had shouted. There across the front yard was a big burly black-haired man bending over someone.

Larry had heard the shout and had seen the man immediately. He and the sheriff ran toward the man…the sheriff leading the way with his gun drawn.

"Halt! Hold on there!" He ran briskly through the snow and fired a shot into the air as the man whirled quickly and disappeared into the trees. Bob was not far behind, and he stopped to see about Mrs. Jamison as Larry and the sheriff followed the stranger out of sight.

"Get on the sheriff's radio and call for an ambulance!" Bob shouted to Jerry Davis as he came running from the other car. He did not hesitate and turned quickly back to the police car.

Bob was kneeling beside the small woman. At first, he thought she was dead. She was very cold and pale. He lifted her tiny wrist and felt for her pulse. There was a very weak heartbeat. He took off his coat and laid it over her.

Jerry had taken the keys from the police car and had gotten two wool blankets from the trunk. He hurried up to Bob, panting heavily. Together, they folded one into thirds and lay it on the snow. Then they very carefully moved her onto it and tucked the other blanket around her.

Bob was feeling nervous and angry, and he shuddered to think what he knew. He was sure the man they had seen just now was the same man he saw last fall in the woods. He was sure also that the sheriff had come to the same conclusion, because of the knowing look he gave Bob when they saw this man kneeling over Mrs. Jamison.

"How could we have let this thing go so far?" Bob had muttered. "We should have looked until we found this killer."

"What did you say, Bob?" Jerry had asked.

"Oh, I'll tell you later. Here comes the ambulance." He got up and motioned for it to pull around the other cars and up near them.

"Hurry," he called. "She's still alive!"

Immediately, the trained attendants had begun their life saving techniques. They worked quietly and efficiently while Bob and Jerry stood watching helplessly.

After many long agonizing moments, one of the attendants pulled a white sheet over her body. Bob's heart sank as he pulled it up over her pallid face. He turned to the two men standing there with their hats in their hands.

"I'm sorry. I guess she was just hurt too badly," he said as they lifted her into the ambulance. They heard shouting from the woods. The sheriff and Larry came running out, quite out of breath.

"Jerry, will you call around and have someone bring some horses over here?" He gasped, holding his side. "We could have never caught him on foot!" He paused, taking several deep breaths. "Land sakes alive, he must be half wolf!"

"What about Mrs. Jamison?" Larry asked as he stood straight, beginning to breathe easier. "Is she alright?"

Jerry had hurried to the car, and Bob shook his head solemnly. "She was still alive when we got here, but she didn't make it," He wiped at his eyes with the back of his hand. "Dear God, we *have* to catch him!"

Soon the four men started down the trail the two women had taken the evening before. They knew this stranger had been up to something there in the woods. Earnestly they hoped to find a clue to what had taken place.

***

Bob and the sheriff were working silently, scratching the earth and snow back with their gloved hands. Before long, Bob could feel something there that he could tell was not earth.

"Sheriff," he said, raising his head as Larry and Jerry joined them there in the woods. "I think I have found something… it is sort of soft… looks like cloth." He looked at Larry and suddenly they knew what was buried there.

"It's a body," Jerry whispered. He stepped a little closer and knelt on the ground beside Bob.

"It sure is," the sheriff agreed, "and it looks like it has been here quite a while."

"Oh, Dear God!" Larry cried in anguish. "It's Jill! That murderer buried her here!" He fell to his knees and all four men worked frantically to uncover the remains of the body. Snow was falling now and freckling their bent backs.

Moments later, they had the job done, and Larry stood up and walked away from the grizzly scene. He was sobbing quietly, but it was relief he felt, not the agony of grief. After close examination they knew the body was not Jill's…it was that of a man!

Chapter 20

It was all a bad dream…a nightmare. Andy had been making his rounds as usual when he came upon the Widow Watson's place. As he came over the hill, he saw her and another woman walking along the path by the river. After they were out of sight, he had gone on down past the chicken house toward the root cellar. He noticed with a grin that she had unlocked it and he knew it was for him. He would help himself to a few carrots and onions and perhaps another jar of those delicious pickles.

In his bag, he carried a generous amount of wild hickory nuts and chestnuts to leave for her. He took his time, examining all the treasures and pleasures of Mrs. Watson's root cellar. He thought this was his most favorite place to be…perhaps it was that mixture of food smells and cinnamon. The sweet smell lingered with him for hours after having been there. He saw that there were some eggs and butter and he could already taste them. She had left an axe head next to the food on a small table in the middle of the room. The handle had splintered and broken only inches from the head and he knew she wanted him to make another handle.

He was placing the axe head in his bag with the other things when he heard someone outside. He lifted his head and listened. Someone was in trouble out there and he feared it was Mrs. Watson. Automatically, he reached up and pulled the string to turn off the light.

Then the scream that made him move was ear piercing and he raced up the cellar steps three at a time, leaving his bag on the table. Just as his shoulders were out of the door, he saw a man's face. A face he knew he had seen before. It was too late, and before he could react, the heavy door of the cellar was shoved forcefully onto his head. He fell backwards down the steep steps and into oblivion.

He awakened and did not know where he was. It was dark and he thought he was blind. His head throbbed so that he could not move, and then he was unconscious again. Hours later, he awoke a second time. There was light coming in around the door. Enough so that the big man could tell where he was and he remembered why he had come here. But why had he slept?

He felt much better and after a few minutes was able to stand. He pulled the string and turned on the light. Walking gingerly over to the table he took the canteen from his bag. He took a long drink, thinking how grateful he was to Widow Watson for giving it to him many years ago.

Then it came to him…she was hurt!! He had to help her! He hurried up the steps, but went more cautiously this time. He did not notice the throbbing in his head now as he slowly pushed up on the heavy door. He did not know if it would open, but it did, creaking all the way.

Carefully, he looked all around before pushing it back against the stop. He could not see anything or anyone until he was completely out of the cellar. Then he saw her. Her body lay crumpled behind the door stop. Rushing to her, he saw right away that it was not Widow Watson; she was much too small. He was sure it must be the woman he watched walk away with her yesterday.

He closed the cellar door to take the shadow away. He could tell she was still alive and he gently lifted her like a sleeping child and moved her away from the cellar. He knelt down to listen to her heart when he heard someone shout.

He knew they were thinking he had done harm to this poor lady, and when he saw the sheriff's gun, he was afraid they would not listen to him deny it. He made an instant decision to get away as fast as possible. He winced when he heard the gunshot and was more convinced than ever that he had better run fast because they were going to shoot him for something he didn't do. So, he ran… like he had never run before.

***

The nightmare was terrifying… running… ever running! He awakened again. Someone had him by the shoulder, shaking him gently.

"Uncle Andy, Uncle Andy! Are you alright?" Jill leaned over him where he had collapsed onto his bed in the cave. Tears ran down her face as she told her terrible story of searching for him and thinking he had taken the horse from a little girl in the forest.

"But you didn't do that, I just know you didn't." He patted her hand silently and nodded for her to continue her tale. She told of finding the mess in the woods and of the blood on the trail. She cried openly when she admitted that she thought it might be his blood.

She was exhausted and laid her head on her crossed arms on the side of his bed and wept. Uncle Andy patted her shoulders as they heaved with hard sobs. He waited.

Finally, she raised her head and with tears on her face, she looked deep into his eyes. "What happened to you last night?" She asked slowly, with a sobbing hiccup. "I was so worried about you. So scared!"

He gently pushed her back a bit so that he could sit on the edge of the bed. As he started up, he grabbed his head with both hands. The pain was a terrible one. It's a wonder I'm still here, he thought.

"Oh, Uncle," she shrieked. "You did get hurt! Is it okay? Can I get you something?" She stood up, looking urgently around trying to decide what she could do for her friend.

""I'm fine. Just took a bump on the head. I'll tell you all about it later. Could you make us a fresh pot of coffee, and I will find us something to eat."

She looked at him impatiently. "But, Uncle…" she began. He raised a thick hand to silence her and moved slowly toward the woodstove. "It's a long story, little One, and I will tell you all about it. But first, we need to eat and get you settled down. Remember, we must think about your health. All this excitement can't be too good for you."

Jill prepared the coffee pot and moved to the entrance of the cave. "It's starting to snow," she said absently as she stood there with her hands in the pockets of her jeans. She remembered the small wooden statue being in the pocket of her coat and went to get it.

"Ohhh…" she moaned tragically, as she frantically searched the pockets. "Your statue's gone. I must have lost it!" Turning toward him, she put her hands over her face and started to weep again.

Uncle Andy put down the knife he was using to cut the bread and moved to her side. Putting his arms around her, he held her close to him as she cried out her anguish. His heart ached for her.

In a bit, she said against his shoulder, "I saw Larry today. Oh, Dear God!" She sobbed all the harder.
After a few more moments, she lifted her head and looked into his face, searching it with her swollen eyes. "Did you know something awful happened to the Widow Watson? I saw them putting her in the ambulance and she was, oh, she was dead!" Her knees went out from under her as she lost consciousness.

138

Andrew picked her up and carried her to the bed, gently laying her down. He covered her with a quilt and moved around the cave preparing soup and hot tea for her. Then he wet a cloth in cool water and sat down on the edge of her bed.

"Oh, Little One," he said softly, "you have been through so much these past months. Dear God," he prayed earnestly, "give her strength. Help me know what to do."

He tenderly bathed her face and talked softly to her until she was fully awake.

"Uncle Andy? What…" She began.

"Shhh, Little One, just rest," he crooned. "I want you to take some of this soup and then you are going to sleep. We can talk later," he said quietly in a firm voice. Gently, he stroked her forehead.

Jill was so tired and weak that she just nodded and let him spoon feed her the warm broth. She sipped the hot tea, letting its heat soothe her tired body. She went to sleep remembering his sensitive, gentle touch. It was the same as when she first came to him.

Chapter 21

It was well after dark and having eaten supper, Bob sat at his table with Old Jack and Pete Greer. The two old gentlemen had come over earlier in the day to be with Doc Jamison as he tended Widow Watson. She had insisted on staying there until they heard some word about her dear friend, Marie.

The news had come much sooner than they expected. Tom Martin had returned to his store an hour after Larry left to join the search for Mrs. Jamison. Mary told him what had been happening and he saddled up his horse and Larry's and went straight to Mrs. Watson's place. Just before he arrived, the phone call had come, requesting horses for the search.

Soon he was there, and could see no one around. He started to call out, but Bob came out of the woods at that moment. They saw each other at the same time.

"Oh, Tom, I'm sure glad you're here. It's beginning to snow, and we need to get after that man right away!" He paused to wipe perspiration off his forehead and out of his eyes. He took a deep breath as he replaced his cap.

"You'll never guess what we found out there in the woods!" He shook his head and walked briskly toward the police car with Tom at his side. Before Tom could answer, Bob stopped and looked at him. "A man's body! It was buried in a shallow grave, and has been there a long time. Poor Larry… we all thought it was Jill at first."

He opened the door of the police car and sat down. Soon he had made the call for someone to come and get the body. It would have to be taken into Drayton for identification and to determine the cause of death.

"Bob," Tom said, just as Bob closed the car door. "What about Mrs. Jamison? Did you did you find her?"

Bob took his stocking cap off again and ran his fingers through his hair. "Yeah, we did, but Tom, she is dead. The ambulance already took her."

He told Tom what had happened to her, and all about the stranger and their unsuccessful chase. Then he rubbed his flushed face and said, "It's gonna kill Doc to lose his mother this way."

"Bob, if you want, you can use my horse and take Larry's to him. I will go back to your place and tell Doc." Tom had been fishing buddies with him for many years and the doctor had been a real friend when Tom's sons were found dead.

"Just tell Larry I took his car. It will be at the store later, whenever he brings the horses back. I don't expect you will be able to follow any tracks for long, the way this snow is falling," he said, blinking the snow from his eyes as he looked into the heavy sky.

"I'm beginning to wonder if we will ever find this killer. He probably killed my boys," he said, swallowing a lump trying to come up in his throat. "And I'm sure he has Jill buried out there somewhere, too."

Tom tried to control the anger in his voice, and shoved his hands into his pockets, leaving his shoulders hunched in despair. "Then there is Jerry's little niece lying in a hospital, too." Clearing his throat, and shuffling his feet, he said, "Well, I'd best be going. I know the Doc is anxious." As an afterthought, he turned to Bob, "If anyone needs me I will be with him. I'll call Mary when I get to your place and tell her."

***

Every moment Tom had taken to drive to Bob's little log cabin was filled with dread. With the Widow

Watson hurt and having to hear this terrible news, he knew it would not be easy.

A miserable hour passed after his arrival, as he told those waiting all he knew. Then he had helped Doc Jamison carry Widow Watson to the car and the three drove to the doctor's house. It seemed to help the Doc to have someone needing his care and he devoted his full attention to consoling her and being a good doctor. They all knew his grief would come later, when he was alone to fully realize his loss.

Susan moved around her kitchen now, filling the coffee cups for the three who sat there. Bob was telling Pete and Old Jack of their fruitless search through the snowy forest.

"We followed his trail and it was really weird. There were horse tracks in the same trail as if it were following him, too. And you know what? When we saw that horse, Jerry was sure it was the same one he had given little Bonnie!" He sipped his coffee and looked at Old Jack as he said, "Maybe this man has an accomplice. What do you think?"

"I don't know, it sure is possible, though. I do know one thing. At least we know what this man looks like now, and we *have* to stop him!" Bob put sugar in his steaming coffee, and stirred it thoughtfully as the three sat in silence.

"Bob?" Susan said, as she turned from the stove. "Was that body anywhere near where you found little Bonnie?" She wiped absently at the table with a damp cloth.

"Yeah, it was," Bob looked up suddenly at her. He raised his eyebrows and looked from Old Jack to Pete.

"Do you suppose Bonnie saw him messing with the body that day?" Pete said, taking a long hot drink of coffee. "Mmm, good coffee, Susan," he said, setting the cup down, cradling it in his work worn hands. He absently twisted it back and forth.

Susan smiled at the bearded old man and turned to Bob. "Why would he go back there? Twice?"

Before Bob could answer, Old Jack said, "The twins, they were fishing along there last summer when they disappeared, weren't they?"

"Dear God," Susan said, leaning against the edge of the table, "Could they have seen him kill that poor man in the grave?" A chill went up her spine and she shivered, clutching her arms across her stomach. She knew that it could have been Randy as well as the twins if this was what had happened that day.

"What gets to me," Bob said, without answering her, "is how this weather seems to stay on his side. This makes the second time it helped him to get away." He stared morosely into his cup. "If he killed the twins and Marie for seeing him with that body and tried to kill Bonnie and Widow Watson? And…well, I'm sure Jill is buried out there, too. How many more will he hurt before he's through?"

Bob was thinking out loud until now. He sat staring into his cup and the only sounds in the room were the crackling fire in the wood stove and the hiss of falling snow against the hot stove pipe.

Chapter 22

In the wee hours of the morning, far away in the white forest, Andy made quiet preparations to leave his little cave-home. He had arisen very early, feeling rested, but extremely uneasy about the events of the previous day. He knew the lawman thought he had killed that little old lady and that he would soon have everyone out looking for him. He feared for Jill's safety and moved around the cave silently so that he would not disturb her sleep. He would leave, and she would be found later on by the search parties he knew would come. She would be better off going back home than staying with him and very possibly being in danger.

He already knew where he would go. It was a long trip on foot or horseback, and was high in the mountains. He felt he would never be found there and had doubts whether he would ever come back to this area. He felt great sorrow at never seeing Little Jill again, but he knew this had to be done.

With a heavy heart he mechanically packed his things. Occasionally, he would glance at Jill's sleeping face and would have to choke back a lump in his throat. To keep from thinking about losing his little friend, he thought about his plans for his new life. He had been there before, many years ago. In fact, it was the place where he first set foot in these mountains. He had amazing memories of the details and location.

He was only fifteen years old then... an orphan who had been in the home of an aunt and uncle for a big part of his young life. That had not worked out well at all, and finally he had been placed in an orphanage at age ten. He had been there only a short time when he first met Peter. A twenty year old young man, he was the first close friend Andy had ever had. As Andy thought about

Peter it brought his friend Rachel to mind. They were his only true friends until Jill. Peter had died at age twenty-five, and dear Rachel was dead also.

Well, that is all in the past, Andy told himself. He certainly wanted to keep Jill safe so that nothing could happen to her, too.

He tried to visualize the site of the plane crash. Yes, he was sure he could find it again and he was just as sure that everything would still be there.

The day of that plane crash had changed Andy's life. He and Peter had taken the little plane and started across the mountains. Their plan was to land on a remote lake deep in the wilderness, where they were going moose hunting.

They would camp out for two weeks and had plenty of extra supplies on board. One never knew when weather might delay their departure at the end of a trip. They had done this before and had spent hours together hunting, fishing, and just being friends. Peter did not have any family either, and when he and Andy met, he devoted most of his free time to the boy.

Peter had his own plane and pilot's license and had been teaching Andy the fundamentals of flying. They had been enjoying their flight immensely that day. Late in the evening, they ran into a severe early snow storm.

Andy could remember how nervous he had felt as the plane tossed and bumped in the high winds. The snow had been blinding, and when Peter began to realize he no longer had control he hurriedly instructed Andy how to protect himself from injuries during the crash he knew was imminent.

Moments later, they sat in stunned silence as they realized they were alive and absolutely uninjured! Then, they looked at each other for a long moment, and suddenly Peter began to laugh. Avoiding the reality of their plight and out of sheer relief, the two young men threw their heads back and laughed until the tears came.

Andy smiled as he remembered how ridiculous that had been. Love for his friend swept over him again, as it had many times over the years. He swallowed hard as he filled his back pack.

After Peter died in the log cabin fire, Andy had gone back to the site of the plane crash. They had left all their gear in the rear of the plane where it seemed inaccessible because of the position of the airplane and the extremely deep snow.

With an axe he had picked up from the woodpile as he left the log cabin, he spent many hours prying and chopping. Finally he was able to get into the storage compartment and retrieve all of the food and gear that he and Peter had carefully packed weeks before. He could remember weeping bitterly as he unpacked everything. He spread it all out to see just what he had to rely on.

Peter was dead and Billy, the old mountain man, had burned in the fire along with him. Andy would never forget how Billy had rescued them from entrapment in the plane days after the crash. They had managed to survive by rationing the box of chocolate bars and peanuts they had carried in the cockpit.

Peter had gotten his window open a little ways and was able to get an occasional handful of snow for them to swallow. They had been forced to stay in the plane that night because of the severe snow storm. They never even knew when it ended, as the whole front end of the plane was covered in deep snow. Soon they lost track of the days and nights.

It was only by chance that Billy found them. He was tracking a wounded fox that had escaped one of his traps and the tracks led within feet of the tail of the plane. Billy could not imagine what it was at first. He walked all around the plane in his snow shoes, mumbling to himself.

"What on earth *is* this?" He was standing on top of the plane, scratching his head, as he spoke aloud. His surprise when he heard a commotion below him, made him tumble down the "hill". Soon he had enough snow scooped back to see that there were people inside a small plane! He worked frantically as the two inside shouted, laughing and crying with joy. They had felt sure they were spending their last hours in this life.

"Hold your horses! I'm comin'!" The grizzled old man mumbled as he worked.

When they heard the old trapper mumbling and then fully realized that they were saved, the old man looked like an angel of mercy to them. His weathered old face beamed as he pulled them out, one by one. They collapsed into a heap on the snow, as their legs were too weak to support them.

Billy had built a fire and given the two comrades hot black coffee in a single steel cup. Then he shared the dried jerky that he carried in his small day-pack. After a while, they were able to start out for Billy's cabin. They stopped often to rest, as the two men were extremely weak from their ordeal.

Finally, they reached the cabin, and Peter and Andy had never felt happier than they did that day. They slapped each other on the back as they laughed and celebrated their rescue. The small cabin smelled of bacon and tobacco as the warm air rushed out when the door was opened. They quickly stomped the snow from their feet and Billy helped them inside and made them comfortable on animal skins he spread out on the floor near the stove. He built up the fire and prepared a hot meal for the men. Before it was ready, though, they were both deep in an exhausted sleep, oblivious to the bugs crawling in the animal skins.

Andy smiled again as he remembered how he felt waking up hours later with bugs all over him. It was morning and he couldn't believe he was actually stretched out, resting, rather than cramped into a sitting position. Even the bugs were better than what they had been through.

They had been with Billy for a few short weeks when the tree fell through the cabin roof. It was a huge, snow-laden pine tree which had leaned precariously on the side of the hill over the cabin for years. Its twin stood straight and tall in contrast.

The crash upset the lantern and the whole place was in flames within moments. Andy could not remember how he got out of there that night. He had seen Billy trapped beneath the tree, unconscious as the flames licked at his face.

Peter had been across the room and Andy could still hear him calling his name. He ran frantically all around the outside of the cabin, sobbing and shouting Peter's name over and over. He was devastated that he could not see a way to get Peter out. Helplessly, he could hear him calling, and finally, he just turned and ran, with his hands over his ears. He ran stumbling, and ran and ran as falling slow pelted him in the face, melting into the trails of tears there. He had to get away… he could not bear to hear his friend dying…

***

"Andy? Uncle Andy? What's wrong?" Jill was up out of bed, standing beside him as he sat with his head in his hands. She put her hand on his shoulder and sat down beside him.

148

He looked up at her, tears still streaming down his face. "Little One, I have to leave. I am going way up in the mountains and I will never be back. I want you to wait here until the lawman comes and then you must go home." Suddenly, he stood, took her in his arms and held her tightly.

"I love you, Jill. You have been like the daughter I know I will never have. Always remember that," he said.

Then he held her at arm's length and looked into her face. He started to say more, but she put her fingers over his mouth to silence him.

"You know I love you, too, Uncle Andy. But if you go, I'm going with you. We belong together and I won't stay unless you do," she said, her tears beginning to fall.

She knew why he felt he must go, and she feared for him. She was afraid that he would be accused of killing that lady, and because they had the little girl's horse, they might think he did that, too. She still did not know how he got the horse, but she just knew he did not hurt that little girl.

"Don't you think they would believe you if you just tell them you didn't do it?" Jill wiped her eyes with the back of her hand and stepped over to the water can. Taking a drink of water from the dipper she looked up at the big man. As she turned to replace the dipper, she saw his bulging pack by the entrance of the cave. Before he could answer her question, she turned to him and cried, "You were going to leave without telling me, weren't you? Oh, why? Why?" She covered her face with her hands and sobbed.

Andy moved to her side and put his arms around her. "Please, Little One, don't cry. I thought it would be easier not to have to say goodbye. I didn't want to hurt

149

you, and I didn't want to have you try to make the long journey. Please, try to understand," he pleaded.

She jerked away from him and moved across the cave. She started gathering her few belongings together. Angrily, she threw them on her bed.

"I am going with you," she insisted. "I will be okay! I can't go home now, they already think I'm dead and I can't put them through that again! Besides, you need me…" and as her anger subsided, she turned to him saying, "and I need you!" She rushed back across the cave and into his arms. He lifted her off the floor in one of his bear hugs and laughed heartily.

"Okay, you win! You can go with me, feisty gal!" Putting her down, he went on with his packing. After a moment, he said, "I was planning on leaving the little horse so it could be returned when you went home, but since you are going with me, I think we ought to take him, don't you? You can ride some that way and won't have to walk so much. It will be a very long journey."

"I guess you are right, Uncle. Besides, if we leave him they will be convinced you hurt that little girl and I know you didn't!" She stopped packing food and looked at him. "Will you tell me how you *did* get Ebony?"

"Sure, Honey. I found him wandering in the forest. I didn't know where he came from and didn't see anyone around at all. I know I shouldn't have taken him, but I just knew you would love him. After all, it was Christmas, and I wanted the perfect gift."

He looked down at the ground as he finished. He had felt guilty about taking the animal ever since that day. He had done it on the spur of the moment and had had regrets about it, especially after seeing the newspapers telling about the little girl who was hurt. The truth that he did not quite know what to do about it.

Relief flooded through her body and with a small smile, Jill silently returned to her work. She had known of his innocence, but now that it was spoken, it was all she needed to give the man her loyalty.

Soon they had a backpack fixed up for her and he wore his. They slung two large bags of food behind the saddle. They moved the horse a short distance away from the cave and then went back to do what they could do to disguise the area. They placed snowy branches and bushes in front of the entrance after getting the blankets out. Jill folded them into rectangles and draped them across the saddle. She could sit on them and would hardly know they were there.

The partial crisscross style corral was disassembled easily in just a few moments, and Andy spread the long logs on the ground and kicked snow over them. It was very early, long before daylight and the snow still fell heavily. They were grateful for the thick blanket of snow they knew would hide their traces very quickly as long as it continued to fall.

They never looked back as Andy led the horse and Jill followed. She wanted to walk, at least for a while. She was too keyed up to sit idly on the back of a horse. They were headed for a new life up there...and she did not know what kind of life it might be. She just knew she trusted this man implicitly, and now that they shared the Lord as their Savior, she had complete confidence in his ability to care for her.

It did not even seem important to know she would never come back. That part of her life was in the past and in God's hands. She looked with hope to what lay ahead.

Chapter 23

About ten o'clock that morning, everyone could hear the church bell ringing loud and clear in the still air. It was not Sunday, and those who had not heard about Marie Jamison's death knew now that there was to be an important meeting...a town crisis had occurred.

They came in cars, pickups, on foot, and on horseback. The people congregated on the front lawn of the church building and soon the news had spread to each who was there.

Snow had fallen throughout the night and continued, peppering the heads and shoulders of the townspeople as they gathered. The crowd talked quietly in front of the church, each shocked and distressed at the continuing tragedies.

It had been a long and anxious night for the sheriff and the other men who had waited for the news from Drayton where the man's body had been taken for identification.

Searchers had followed the double tracks until they split off in opposite directions. So the men formed two groups, and each followed a trail until darkness and deep snow put a stop to their efforts. They had agreed to meet back at the sheriff's offices so they went there and discovered that the dead man had been taken away. Each went home exhausted but very hopeful that they would find out what this was all about when the body could be identified.

So now, hearing the church bell, they rushed away from home and chores and jobs, their one thought was to know who the dead man was and how he fit into the things that had happened.

Faye Miller, Larry's mother, and his two sisters, Linda and Brenda, stood with the women watching the sheriff and some of the other men quietly discussing something in very low voices.

"Mother," Linda began, shivering in the cold, "do you think it is ever going to end?" Her pale young face was strained and there were dark circles under her eyes from anxiety and loss of sleep. She pulled her coat and scarf tighter around her neck, leaving her hands clutched at her throat.

Faye gently put her arm around her frail daughter, and Brenda moved to her sister's other side and together they felt somehow to be protecting her. Linda had always been tiny and easily exhausted. Asthma had taken its toll on her weak system, and today her breathing was very difficult in the cold air.

"Linda, dear, I do wish you would've stayed home by the fire. We could've let you know as soon as we heard anything." Faye squeezed her daughter's shoulders and reached to straighten her warm hat where it tilted over to one side. She cleared her throat and continued in a reassuring voice, "Of course it will end. In fact, I'm sure it must be almost over now. They have seen the killer and from what Larry says, they may be able to find fingerprints on the... what was it?" She turned and looked at Brenda, raising her thin eyebrows.

"It was a crowbar, Mama, and if they do find prints on that, Linda, that will be that and they'll catch him in no time. Just wait and see!" She smiled reassuringly at her, nodding to her mother. Her bright eyes flashed as the tassel on her hat bobbed up and down.

"Oh, sure, and I'm the President of the United States, too," sneered Bones Jones, elbowing his way closer to hear their conversation. His real name was Clarence, but he was such a tall, extremely thin man that he had acquired the nickname Bones as a teenager, twenty years ago. He was a cynical, hard man who could never

153

find anything good about anyone or anything. He worked at the saw mill with Bob, where his stamina and strength alone kept him his job. He was a very unpleasant person to be around, but he never missed a day at work and was ruthlessly dependable and never late. He lived alone off in the woods in a little shanty, openly bitter over hard times in his life.

"I'm tellin' you, that killer will keep on killing and we'll never see the likes of him again!" He smugly crossed his arms and stood there with his narrow jaw firmly set and his thin lips pressed tightly together. His small head sat arrogantly on top of his long neck.

"Why do you say that, Bones?" Faye demanded, holding Linda even tighter.

"You'll see…you'll see," he said, tucking his absent chin in as far as it could go. He stared ahead toward the sheriff who was making his way toward the steps of the church.

"Attention! May I have your attention?" The sheriff spoke loudly to be heard above the murmurings of the crowd. As they quieted, he took off his hat and ran his fingers through his hair. He put it back on, and hitching up his pants, began to speak.

"Folks, I'm sure by now most of you have heard what happened just yesterday."

"You bet we did!" shouted Bones Jones, "And what are you doing about it is what I want to know!"

"Hold your horses, Bones, and I'll tell all of you," the sheriff held his hand up to silence the impudent man.

"Now, first of all, I'm a knowin' you all will like to hear that the Widow Watson is gonna be fine." He continued above their relieved murmurs, "and you'll all be glad to know that Jerry's little niece, Bonnie, has come out of her coma, and we hope to be able to get a statement from her any day now!"

154

Susan took her son's and daughter's hands and squeezed them tightly, as tears filled her eyes. She had prayed many times for little Bonnie and had stayed up all last night praying for the Widow Watson. Over and over she quoted Scriptures from God's Word, drawing strength from Him. Her children had heard her prayers, and looked at one another now with love and gratitude in their eyes.

Jill's mother, Joan Clark, stood silently with her husband Frank. He had his arm protectively about her shoulders. Mary Martin was at her other side holding tightly to her hand. Quietly they listened as the sheriff continued.

"Doc's mother, Mrs. Jamison, has been killed, and well…I know you are all as sad about that as I am," the sheriff stopped and wiped his hands across his face and took a deep breath. "Our Doc sure didn't deserve that to happen," he said, his voice cracking with emotion. He cleared his throat with difficulty.

"Now," he continued in a more businesslike way, "now, we do have some incriminating evidence and some clear fingerprints. Plus, we know the identity of the dead man we found buried in the woods."

The crowd began talking excitedly, but Sheriff Billings just spoke louder and continued to talk. Quickly, the crowd quieted as he said, "Do you remember a while back when that Henry Dumas was killed over at the saw mill?"

"Well, I sure do!" The loud screechy voice startled people nearby. "I saw it happen! Stupid man could've killed me, too, if I hadn't been fast as lightning!" Bones spoke up, obviously proud of his agility. "What's that got to do with it, anyhow?"

"Shhh!" The command came from all over the crowd. People were irritated at the rude interruptions.

Shooting his eyes at Bones, the sheriff continued. "Anyway, this Henry Dumas was wanted in a burglary, and it seems the dead man in the woods there was his partner, Jake Purcell. Now, at the time of the burglary, there were witnesses who had eventually identified Purcell and Dumas from mug shots, but there was a third partner, who has as yet remained unidentified. I'm thinking our killer just may have been that third partner.

"You see, about the time of the Martin twins' disappearance… 'Scuse me, Tom, Mary," he added respectfully, nodding his head toward them where they stood at the side of the steps.

"About that time, there was a man disappeared from over at Drayton. Well, that man was this Purcell that we found buried in the woods. Now we don't have any proof that this has any bearing on what may have happened that day to the twins, or not, but we will be doing our best to find out."

Again the crowd started talking excitedly, bewildered and perplexed at what they had heard.

"Please, there's more," the sheriff said, raising his hand toward the people.

"Seems like this killer really likes his self, because right near the grave we found a small carving, a statue of the killer. I'm still amazed about finding such a thing," he said, shaking his head and thrusting his cold hands into his coat pockets.

"Now, this is what the killer looks like. He's a big man with black hair and beard and according to Widow Watson, his face is terribly scarred from a fire or something. When we saw him yesterday, he wore a green army jacket and blue jeans."

"I knew it! I knew it!" Bones Jones was shouting, slapping another man on the back in glee.

"Now, see here, Bones, I've had about enough out of you," the sheriff began but Bones loudly continued.

"I've seen him! I've seen him hunderds of times!" The thin man was becoming very excited, the spittle flying out of his small mouth. He moved swiftly toward the sheriff, wiping his chin with the back of his hand.

"What do you mean, seen him? Where?" Sheriff Billings stood with his hands on his hips, not knowing what Bones was up to now.

"Well, it all started years and years ago. Lots of old folks back in them hills know about the 'mountain man'. Oh, most have never seen him, but I have," he stuck his thumbs in his belt loops, pulling his shoulders back importantly, watching the reaction of the baffled crowd.

"Come on, man, tell what you know," urged Deputy Bill, stepping from behind the sheriff to see if he could tell by this strange man's face if he were telling true.

"Okay!" Bones sneered at the deputy. "Give me time, will ya?" Turning to face the crowd, Bones drawled, "Fer years there's been this *real* mysterious man sneaking around taking things from folks in the hills. Yep," he grinned at their puzzled faces, enjoying being the center of attention. "He's real mysterious… lurking around, waitin' til ain't no one lookin' and then he scoots right up, bold as brass and takes things! Why, I even seed him take one of my chickens…just snuck right up and grabbed it by the neck, he did."

"Why didn't you stop him?" Bob Greyson spoke up, trying very hard not to be irritated with this hard man.

"Didn't want to, that's why! Wanna know why? Cuz he allus leaves somethin' and I like s'prizes!" He rocked back on his heels, enjoying himself. "Sometimes

157

he leaves me fruit or nuts, fresh from the woods, and sometimes cheese. I never know what, but he never takes somethin' that he don't leave somethin' behind. I even got to where I'd put certain things out for him, and most of the time he'd take what I put out for him."

Bones attitude seemed to be changing as he talked, realizing that if his mountain man were indeed the killer, he would be denied the pleasure of watching the mysterious stranger. His voice trailed away. He swallowed repeatedly, his adam's apple bobbing up and down in his long neck.

"Has anyone else seen this 'mountain man'?" Sheriff Billings said, looking out over the crowd, his eyes stopping for a brief knowing glance at Bob.

"I've had things took from my place in the hills," Hannah Edwards spoke up, pushing her way toward the steps of the church.

"It has been right strange, but like Bones here says, he always leaves somethin' in return. It ain't really stealin' is it?"

"Well, I don't rightly know, Mrs. Edwards," spoke the sheriff gently, taking the old lady by the elbow as she struggled up the steps.

"Have you seen him at all?" he asked her, brushing the snow from her stooped shoulders.

"No… well, not exactly. That is, I saw his back oncet, and he was a big man. I always thought it was kinda fun havin' things come and go. I'd put out a big piece of chocolate pie and a can of coffee or somethin', and he'd leave me a bag of apples or somethin'. Sheriff," she said, looking beseechingly up into his eyes, "he even fixed my barn door one time when I wasn't to home. Now could someone like that be a killer?" Tears began splashing down Hannah's face and she looked down at the Doctor, shaking her head. "I guess it could have been me, too, Doc, right along with your poor mother. I'm so sorry I never said nothin'."

The sheriff gently placed his arm around Hannah's small shoulders and indicated to Deputy Bill to help her down the steps.

"Mrs. Edwards, can you stay after the meeting and come into my office for a talk?" he asked, touching her on the arm.

"Sure, if you think it will help," she replied, as she slowly stepped toward the crowd.

"You too, Bones, and anyone else here that might know something of this 'mountain man'. He sure is vain and egotistical to carve a statue of his own self, and we must get to the bottom of this!"

Chapter 24

The sheriff had dismissed the crowd, keeping the main search party members with him. Pastor Jordan was still there, but had gone inside the small church, the words of his prayer still resounding within his heart.

As Sheriff Billings moved to call the meeting to a close, Hannah Edwards had asked if the pastor could be allowed to lead them all in prayer. After all, she had pointed out, there are so many things going on and so many people hurting, that they surely needed all the help the Lord could give them.

"Gracious Heavenly Father," Pastor Jordan began, "we come to You in Jesus' dear name, to ask Your blessing upon all these fine people. We ask that You comfort those who are hurt and grieving, and confused by what has happened. Your Word says in Philippians chapter four and verse thirteen, that we can do all things through Christ who strengthens us, and Lord, we ask You to be with each of us and give us strength.

"Dear Lord, we ask You to be with Doc as he's lost his precious mother, and we thank you that our friend, Mrs. Watson will recover, along with dear little Bonnie. We thank You for Your presence that we can draw strength from at this difficult time. We ask Your help for those who are pursuing the investigation so that this can all be brought to a swift end.

"And dear Father, we especially ask You to help the poor deranged man who has caused such grief among our people here."

Bones Jones shifted uneasily and briefly glanced up at the Pastor with unbelief in his hard black eyes. How could he dare ask help for that skum, he thought. He slammed his hat down over his snow covered head and no one saw him leave.

The pastor sat in the front row of the church now, with his head in his hands. He could hear the muffled voices of the men who were gathered under the shelter of the porch outside.

"Now, Bob," Sheriff Billings began, "there's still more that I didn't tell just everybody. You men will all understand why in a minute. First off, Deputy Bill, you go to the office and take a statement from Hannah, Bones, and the others. Meet us out at Bob's place in an hour." Bill hurried away as the sheriff continued.

"Bob, I want you to head up a different type of search party. You, Old Jack, and Pete, and myself will need horses. Larry, you, Tom, and Frank might as well come along, too. Bring day packs and dress warm. In fact, you might all bring a flashlight as it may get on after dark before we come back."

"Where on earth are we going?" Larry, in his youthfulness, could not hide the eagerness and anticipation in his voice.

"I'm coming to that, boy, be patient," the sheriff replied gently, with an understanding smile. He pulled a folded piece of paper out of his pocket and began, "What we have here is a map, found on the body of that Jake Purcell. This here is the reason I'm convinced our killer is the third robbery partner. It gives him a good reason to be digging up the grave and obviously the two ladies prevented him from finding it the other day.

"I'm also thinking that little Bonnie and maybe even Jill prevented him from getting it another time. And seeing as this Jake fella disappeared about the time the twins did, they may have just been in the wrong place at the wrong time. Again, I'm mighty sorry, Tom," he spoke tenderly to the father who winced at his words.

Jill's father, Frank Clark, held his head up and straightened his shoulders when the sheriff looked

161

compassionately into his eyes. Swallowing a lump in his throat, he said, "I don't think I'll go along this time, Sheriff Billings. Joan has been feeling poorly and I don't really want to leave her for long until this thing is settled. If we could only find Jill's body and have a proper funeral I think she'd adjust."

"Sure, Frank," said the sheriff kindly. "I understand, and if you folks need anything, you just let us know."

He removed his hat as he watched Frank turn and go down the church steps. He shook his head and pressed his lips together in a thin line. Then, "Don't know how they're ever gonna make it…" he said sadly.

Then he replaced his hat and looking at the map, said determinedly, "Now, it don't exactly say so, but the 'X' here on this map and the other little notes scribbled here makes me think that we can follow it and go right out there and find the stolen property from the stupid robbery that started this mess in the first place."

"Wow. I can't believe all of this," Tom Martin said, shaking his head. "Some sick man killing four people and hurting countless others just to recover something that never was his in the first place. I just don't understand people like that."

"That's for sure," Old Jack agreed, putting his arm across the shoulders of his friend. He let it lie there as the sheriff continued.

"Now, Bob, the reason I want you to lead out is that according to this here map, the loot is hidden out in the woods north of your place and you're most likely to know that area the best.

"Okay," he said, taking a deep breath and patting Tom on the back. "Let's get going, then. Maybe by morning they will have some information about the prints we found on that there crowbar."

162

In less than an hour the search party had gathered at Bob's little log cabin, horses stamping impatiently in the snow. Susan had prepared two big thermoses of hot coffee and assured the men that she would have a big pot of homemade stew waiting when they returned.

She stood on the porch outside, holding a towel above her face to keep the snowflakes out of her eyes. The snow seems to be letting up now, she thought gratefully. "God, be with them," she said softly as she turned to go inside the warm cabin.

Bob had been only slightly interested when he noticed that the 'X' on the map was in the same general area that he and Randy had gone to find a Christmas tree such a short time ago.

He thought about that day now, as the men rode silently along. The snow was not nearly as deep that day, and he remembered how he and Randy had enjoyed themselves, getting away without "the women" in the family. He smiled, remembering his young son's comment.

After quite some time, they neared the area where the map indicated the loot to be hidden. Leaning in their saddles, Bob and the sheriff examined the map, pinpointing landmarks noted in the margins.

"Well!" exclaimed Bob, pushing his hat back on his head.

"Well, what?" asked the sheriff, looking at Bob quizzically.

"Just a coincidence, I guess," Bob answered, pointing to the map.

"See here, in the margin? It says 'pine tree-lightning'. Well, I think I know that tree. It's just up ahead and to the west a ways. I noticed it had fallen last time I was here."

"When was that?" the sheriff wanted to know.

163

"Christmas Eve. Randy and I came out here for a tree, and we ate our lunch over by that old pine. I remember seeing a baby pine growing there. Funny how you notice little things like that," Bob mused, scratching his head.

The group had continued toward the big pine, at Bob's direction, and each was soon dismounted from his horse. Each man stretched wearily, as they waited for more instructions. Some got shovels off the backs of their horses and were anxious to know where they should dig. Pete and Old Jack had their pick axes ready and shuffled their way through the snow toward where Bob and the sheriff studied the map more closely.

"Well, I'll be...see here," Sheriff Billings said, looking at Bob with a half-smile. "On the bottom it says 'under B.P-planted myself'. Now, what do you suppose that means?"

Bob grinned, "Baby pine! Of course, it's buried under that baby pine tree! Can ya believe that?" He hurried toward the tree with the other men, all glad to know they were close to the end of their search.

Deep snow drifted and covered the enormous tree trunk and there was no sign whatsoever of the baby pine tree, but within minutes, the snow was shoveled away, and rough bark was visible.

"There she is!" shouted Larry with delight as he carefully pushed and kicked the snow from the baby tree, now completely uncovered.

"Okay," said Old Jack with authority. "Let's get more snow scooped aside and me and Pete here, we'll chip and you guys can shovel. Stand aside!"

Axes flew and muscles worked steadily as the two hearty older men hacked away at the frozen earth. In just minutes, the younger men took over to shovel out the loosened soil. The baby pine tree was discarded carelessly without a thought, except for Bob. He walked over beside the sheriff.

"You know, Sheriff, I was planning to watch that little tree grow when I first saw it Christmas Eve," he said, leaning against the warm flank of his horse.

"That was so strange to have seen that and now find out there was loot buried there all the time."

He and the sheriff stood in silent agreement for a moment as they watched the other men hard at work, getting more excited by the minute.

As he thought about that day, suddenly he remembered something else. "Sheriff!" he exclaimed, standing straight and stepping toward him. "I just thought of something!"

"What in the world?" the startled man looked into Bob's eyes, trying to find something there.

The others stopped their digging and glanced over at the two men who stood nearby.

"Remember that the killer had on a red scarf when we saw him?" Bob was unaware that he rushed his words.

"Well, yeah, I remember. Why?" The officer scratched the back of his neck.

"Sheriff, that same day we were here, my red scarf was stolen right off my horse when Randy and I were eating our sandwiches!"

"Why didn't you say something about that before?" the sheriff wanted to know.

"I never really thought too much more about it. You see, we did find tracks, and even followed them for a ways, but they were too small to have been the big man. In fact, I thought so at the time. So, I just decided it was some kid."

Bob went on to tell the sheriff about their theory that the mountain man might have an accomplice.

"You know," Sheriff Billings said thoughtfully, "if that is true, what would he be doing way out here on Christmas Eve?" He said it more to himself than to anyone else.

The others stood with shovels and axes in their hands listening intently to the conversation.

Deputy Bill spoke up, his eyes narrowed with concentration, "You know, it could be that they have a hiding place somewhere out there," he indicated with his free hand. His eyes brightened as he thought of that as a real possibility.

"Yes!" Larry interjected excitedly. "Could be an old cabin or something where they have been hiding while they try to find the map where the loot is. It's strange, now two of the thieves are dead, and the big man doesn't know where the loot is and keeps trying to get the map off the dead body of his partner. Wonder what he's gonna do when he goes back again and finds out the body is gone?" Larry, along with the others there were amazed how things were falling into place now.

The sheriff spoke up, decision in his voice. "Okay, Deputy Bill, take this down. We have to find someone to volunteer to keep watch on the gravesite. First off, we have to stop the story from getting in the papers. Tom you can take care of that for me. And first light tomorrow, we will come back here with more men and divide up and start a search for any possible hiding place.

"For now, though," he said wearily, "let's get that stolen loot dug up and get on back to town…it's really getting late."

Chapter 25

About that time in another town, a little girl lay crying in a dim, quiet hospital room. Softly, her mother crossed the room and took the child in her arms and rocked back and forth crooning gently to her.

"It's going to be alright," the mother said, as her own tears found their way silently down her cheeks. "Everything is going to be alright now."

She knew her young daughter must be remembering the terrifying event that caused her and her family so much grief. Gently she rocked, until eventually the child quieted. She held her a long time that way, neither one speaking, nor feeling the need to.

Outside in the hallway, two men sat quietly together, waiting. Jerry Davis looked comfortingly at his brother, Wes, when they heard the soft crying from inside the room. After a while, they heard soft voices inside and quietly entered the room and stood near the bed as they listened to Bonnie tell her story.

The child smiled sweetly at her Uncle Jerry as she talked about Christmas morning and the beautiful horse he had given her. She talked about how easy the animal had been to control and how she already loved him that morning as they rode along.

After riding quite a while, she noticed someone bending over, a little ways off the side of the path. She got off the horse and watched for a few minutes, wondering who he was and what he might be doing there. He was as close as the other side of the hospital room, she said, and yet he was unaware of her presence. She finally decided he was definitely digging... something she thought to be very strange, knowing the ground freezes as hard as a rock.

"Whatcha doin'?" she asked cheerfully.

The man jerked around, startled into immediate anger. He stammered, "N…nothing! G…go away! Mind your own business!"

"Why are you out here digging? Don't you know the ground is frozen solid? Whatcha got in that hole anyway?" Bonnie pressed in, stepping a little closer.

Frantically, he began covering up the place and became angrier as he worked. "Go away!!" he shouted fiercely.

Hurt and confused by this angry stranger, Bonnie turned dejectedly away, leading the horse. "Okay, okay…" she said softly.

He kicked clean snow over the dirty spot and before she knew it, he was beside her. She looked up at him as he touched her on the arm. She started to pull away, but he spoke gently. His scarred face contorted as he tried to hide his anger.

"Hey, I'm sorry kid. I didn't mean to scare you back there. Would you be a nice little girl and let me borrow your pretty horse," he said, with his mustache quivering in the falling snow. He took her by the arm now, and as she looked him full in the face, smelling his awful breath, she was very afraid. The scars were hideous and his eyes were angry, in spite of his gentle voice.

"No," she said firmly. "I have to go right home." She jerked her arm away and reached for the saddle horn.

The ugly man shoved her down and reached for a dead stump from which he pulled a club. The horse reared in fear as he made the sudden movement. He turned and ran silently through the snow.

"Blackie, come back!" Bonnie yelled, as she tried to get up.

The big man back-handed her. He winced when he heard her head slam against the dead stump as she fell. Snarling through his teeth, he hurled the club toward her where it landed in the snow against her head.

"I guess that'll teach you. I was only gonna scare…," he stammered. "Well, I'm sick of you bratty kids getting in my way, anyhow."

A moment later, she raised her head painfully and looked toward where her beloved horse was running and she saw the man stumbling through the snow behind him.

Then a blessed black veil covered her and she felt no more pain. The next thing she knew, Bonnie told her mother, was waking up in the hospital.

"Uncle Jerry," she spoke through her sobs, "I'm so sorry I lost Blackie. I'm so sorry," she turned her little face into her mother's bosom and wept.

"It's not your fault," Jerry said softly, patting the child gently on her shoulder. "And don't you worry. We'll find your Blackie."

Chapter 26

It was almost dark. The gray sky hung closely like a heavy layer of down. It was bitterly cold, and the wind whistled through the trees. Deep shadows surrounded them.

Andy gently helped Jill down from the exhausted pony, holding firmly to the reins, as Ebony tried in vain to tear away and find some relief from the bitter wind.

"Hang on, fella, we'll get you fixed up in no time." Andy said, as he tied the reins tightly to a thick spruce tree. It offered at least partial shelter from the wind until he could prepare a better place for the weary animal.

He bent his shoulders into the wind, and taking Jill by the hand, he led her carefully into the slight depression against the cliff. There were many evergreen trees all around, and as they stepped out of the wind, she was amazed at how much warmer it seemed already.

"Oh, Uncle, this will be a good place to spend the night, won't it? And look, here is a place where someone had a fire before! Can we build one right away?" Jill's lethargy had been dissolved by the encouragement of shelter from the storm, and she bubbled over with excitement.

Andy had taken off his heavy pack and was already pulling dead branches from the bottoms of the evergreen trees. After shaking the snow from them, he had quite an armful.

Jill gladly helped him arrange them, and he delicately started the pine to burning, using just one match. "You feed the fire and keep it burning while I go out and take care of your little horse," he said, patting her on the shoulder.

Then he added, concern making his voice tight, "Are you feeling alright?"

"Oh, yes, Uncle Andy! I'm already feeling better, just being in out of that wind, and now with this wonderful fire, I'm fine." Jill bustled around, picking up whatever would burn, including a packrat's nest from a corner under a low ledge. "Ewwww!" she said, holding part of it carefully between her thumb and one finger, her arm extended away from her body.

Andy chuckled, and breathed a deep sigh of relief. With a small smile, he pulled his hat down and his collar up tighter around his ears, and went out to face the storm. The cold cut right into his face, and his nostrils felt as though they would freeze shut. He knew the temperature was very low, and the horse needed every extra protection he could prepare for him.

Quickly, he untied the reins, slipping one glove off to aid in the process, and then he led the horse right up into the far side of the shelter from where Jill was building a nice roaring fire. Already its warmth was reflecting from the wall of the cliff. Andy efficiently removed all the gear, along with the saddle and saddle blanket, all the while quietly soothing the animal with gentle words. As he briskly rubbed him down, Jill dug around in one of the packs and found the dry corn they had brought for Ebony.

She also took out a kettle and the coffee pot and quickly filled them with snow and set them on the fire to melt. Soon, after adding more snow, which quickly melted in the warm water, they had hot coffee to warm themselves. There was also a large can of beans warming by the fire. They chewed jerky that Andy had made recently and found their strength renewing as their bodies warmed and rested.

171

"Uncle Andy, I thought we were never going to find a good place to stop. Today seemed even longer than yesterday was." Sitting on a folded blanket with her back against a pack near the cliff wall, she drew up her knees and cupped her hands around the steaming cup of coffee. Shivering inside the blanket she'd pulled around her, Jill recalled the extreme fatigue she had experienced before they had camped that first night. Then she smiled, as she thought of the delight that overcame her when Andy had pulled the little two man tent out of the bottom of his pack.

She hadn't known he had one, and now, she sat pondering over the story he had related to her about his years in the mountains. He told her all about Peter, his best friend who had brought him here and how they had crashed in the airplane Peter was flying. He told her about Billy and the fire that had taken his life, along with Peter's. As they sat huddled in the little tent the night before, they laughed together when he told her about all the bugs in the bedding in Billy's cabin, and they cried together as he related the grief he had experienced when he found himself alone.

He had gone back to the site of the plane crash, running blindly all that night, wild with grief. There, he had been able to eventually overcome the emotions that were paralyzing his very thoughts.

He came to himself, he said, sitting inside the cockpit, shivering from cold and waking from a fitful, exhausted sleep. Later that day as he went through the supplies in the plane, he had found the tent, along with a tarp, sleeping bags, pots, pans, utensils and food. Lots of food!

Jill chuckled aloud as she remembered Andy's face lighting up as he related his delight at finding all that food in the plane. "What are you laughing at, Little

172

One?" Andy was taken from his own thoughts by the sound of her voice.

"Oh, just remembering your telling me how happy you were when you found all that food in the airplane. I can just imagine you…although I can't quite picture what you were like as a teenager! That's younger than I am right now!" She smiled affectionately across the fire at him, and he grinned boyishly at her through his shiny black beard.

Later, as they lay with satisfied stomachs and warm in their pine bough beds, Jill gazed dreamily at the fire. Its long tongues lapped at the large log Andy had found and laid there for the night. The horse softly whinnied and she slightly turned her head to see the sleek animal. Andy had thrown a heavy blanket across the horse's back to keep some of the chill off, and the horse rested now, with his head down and standing on three very tired legs.

She thought again of the nights they had slept in the snug little tent, the same tent in which Andy had spent his first winter in the mountains. He had told her about how he had stretched the tarp across the tent and the open cockpit of the nearby plane, and there he made his home. He used the sheltered area for his fire and cooking, and became very proficient at taking proper care of himself.

He said he had quite enjoyed being alone, as the only person he had ever felt totally comfortable with was gone now. A few weeks after he got settled in and began to accept his situation, he made his way back over the hills to the site of the burned cabin. He felt he owed it to old Billy and to Peter to pay his last respects and put up some kind of marker on the place.

Snow lay heavily on the charred remains of the cabin. He had swallowed past a lump in his throat as he

173

tromped through the deep snow to be able to stand next to the stone chimney which stood valiantly on the spot. He said a few words of farewell to his departed friends, and as he stood there holding the cross he had carved in the evenings by the fire he began to feel a peace steal over him. He told Jill that that day was when he knew there was truly a God out there somewhere that cared for him.

Jill smiled sweetly now, as her eyes closed. She snuggled deeper into the blankets and pulled her hat tighter over her ears. She said a prayer of thanks to her God that she also knew was out there, thankful that He had come to take care of her and her gentle friend.

Chapter 27

Sometime in the night, the howling of the wind stopped. The silence awakened Andy, so he got up and put more wood on the fire, pushing the melted snow water closer so that it would be hot enough for coffee when morning came.

He looked over at Jill who was just a lump under a pile of blankets, and her soft breathing moved them up and down rhythmically. The horse was content now, but the temperature was still very cold. The animal's breath came in white frosty clouds. Andy shivered as he crawled back under his warm covers and tried to find that warm spot he had left.

As he lay there, he thought of the day ahead. He was sure they would arrive at the site of the cabin within a few hours. He wondered if the cross would still be there. He remembered how he had lashed it to the chimney since the ground was frozen and he had had no way to dig. He imagined the spot as it had looked that last time he was there. He felt sure it would be very much the same, as the heavy snow cover would be there as before. Planning the last leg of their journey, he drifted off to sleep.

Morning came with a drastic rise in temperature. Andy could sense it in the very smell in the air. It must be a Chinook, he thought. He always enjoyed these warm January (or February) thaws when they came unexpectedly like this.

He energetically threw off the covers and pulled on his boots. Stoking up the fire, he nudged Jill with his toe. "Little One, wake up! Smell that air! It's gonna be spring for a coupla days, so let's hit the trail!"

Jill peeked out from under the covers at him, enjoying his enthusiasm. Somehow, she could not find enough of her own to match his. She felt like her body was weighted down, so extremely weary. Slowly, she sat up, pulling the blankets around her, and gratefully accepted the coffee he handed her. She took a deep breath, and sipped the hot drink, feeling its warmth all the way down.

"Jill, don't you feel well?"

Andy knelt beside her, feeling her forehead. He straightened her hat which had mostly fallen off while she was sleeping.

"I guess I'm just tired, Uncle Andy. I'm sure it will pass. I just feel so weak today. Don't worry, we do have to get going. You did say we would reach the old cabin site today, didn't you?" She reached out and patted his face and struggled to get to her feet, handing him the half-empty cup.

"That's right," he said cheerfully. "Let's get something nourishing into you right away, and then we'll be off."

They quickly ate their meal, and she folded their bedding while he saddled the horse. In a short time, they were all packed and the fire was carefully put out.

The sun was shining brightly this morning and the spring-like breeze was exhilarating. Jill took a deep breath, and relaxed on the back of the horse as Andy led the way through the deep snow.

Sometimes, he had to take the spade, and shovel snow away so that the horse would not have to struggle so hard with his heavy burden.

After a while, Jill thought she would like to try walking, as she thought it might help her circulation and make her feel better. It was not long though, before she knew she would have to give in and ride again. I just can't get over how weak I have gotten lately, she thought, shaking her head.

176

A couple of times, she felt light headed, like she might faint, but she prayed for God to help it pass, and it did.

"I can do all things through Christ who strengthens me," she quoted silently to herself. Jill found that quoting Scriptures was a very great comfort to her, especially these days. She missed her Bible so much, and she felt the tears come to her eyes as she remembered its soft cover and well-worn pages, marked with her hand at special places.

She wiped her eyes with the back of her glove and sat straighter, trying to shake the fatigue she felt so strongly. She was startled when he yelled.

"Whoopee! That's the big pine, right over there! Can you see it, Jill? It's the twin to the one that fell on the cabin. We're here!"

He turned to grin widely at her and hug the horse's head quickly, and then he pushed on through the deep snow, fairly dragging the weary horse along.

Soon they were closer and could see into the clearing where the little cabin had once stood.

"What?" Andy did not try to conceal the shock in his voice, and Jill alertly followed his gaze. There to her mutual surprise, stood a tiny, snug log cabin. Right under the big pine tree.

"I thought you said it burned? Are you sure we are in the right place?"

Jill tried to control the sudden emotion she was feeling. She so hoped this was the right place.

"Well, yes, Little One, this is the place alright. I couldn't be wrong with so many things still the same. Over there, look, you can see the stream where it comes between those rocks. Almost like a waterfall... see?" He pointed to the myriad of water frozen in place against the stones.

"See that big rock, there, the one with the funny shape? Yep, this is the same place alright… I just don't believe this," Andy said happily.

He hurried forward, leading the horse, as Jill swallowed a lump in her throat. Oh, I pray someone is home, so we can go in and rest and get warm, she thought.

Within a few minutes, they were standing directly in front of the tiny cabin and were in awe of its very presence. It was evident that no one was occupying the dwelling, as snow was drifted over the doorway, and the door was latched from the outside. Shutters were firmly in place over the two front windows, and there was no smoke coming from the stone chimney. Andy tied the little pony to a small hitching rail that was in the front yard and took the spade over to the doorway to scoop enough snow out of the way so that they could get the door open and go inside. There was no lock on the door at all.

In short order, he had the door open and peered into the dark interior. "Jill, bring in what you can carry, and I will get things opened up," Andy said cheerfully as he quickly moved from window to window and opened the shutters, fastening them back with the handy little latches that were there.

Tromping through the deep snow, he went around to the back of the cabin and opened the shutters all the way around. There were six windows in the tiny dwelling. Unbelievable, he thought. Someone really had a thing for windows, he thought with a smile.

Jill filled her arms with blankets and her backpack and struggled through the snow until she came to the doorway, where she, too, peeked inside.

"Anyone home?" she said quietly to the still room. She looked around to see if Andy had heard her, feeling foolish and a bit apprehensive about entering someone else's cabin.

She could see the inside clearly with all the windows opened up, and noticed right away that there were open shutters on the insides of all the windows also. No curtains, she thought. What a novel idea!

She smiled and then sighed deeply as she unloaded her arms in a heap near the doorway. Putting her hands on the small of her back, and stretching, she let her gaze wander around the small room. The first thing she saw was an old black Bible lying on a small table beside an old wooden rocker near a window.

"Oh!" she squealed with delight and rushed across the room. Then she stopped and, putting her hand to her throat, began to talk to her Heavenly Father.

"Father God, how I thank You for this wonderful gift. You never cease to amaze me as You provide for my every need." She gently reached down to wipe the dust from the worn cover, with tears streaming down her pale, drawn face. There was a light there now that had not been there before. Her face almost glowed with its presence.

Ignoring the dust on the seat of the old rocker she sat on the edge of it, carefully opening the pages of the cherished book. She felt like she had been reunited with an old friend. And truly, she had. It wasn't long until she was sitting back and gently rocking as she read the treasured words within.

That was where Andy found her about half an hour later when he brought the rest of the gear into the cabin. He had had quite an interesting experience himself. "Jill, you're never going to guess what I found," he said breathlessly as he rushed into the tiny cabin. He stopped abruptly as he caught sight of the dear little girl who had come to mean so much to him.

179

She raised her radiant face to look at him, expectation and joy written there. He was aware at once of the sun shining in on her through the window, making her whole silhouette seem to glow. He stopped, caught by surprise at the sight she made.

"Well, Uncle Andrew, what is it? Is everything alright?" She gently laid the Bible back on the table, open to the place she had been reading. She stood up, taking an uncertain step toward him, feeling a bit shaky at having risen so fast.

"Yes, Little One, it certainly is alright! But let's get a good hot fire going in the fireplace here and warm this place up. The first thing we have to do is take care of you. I can tell you all about it as we work, okay?" He had piled the rest of their gear on the floor with hers. Now he headed across the room to the ample supply of firewood that was stacked beside the corner fireplace below the well-stocked shelves.

Within a few minutes, he had laid a fire in the clean fireplace and the warmth began to send out its gentle fingers to caress the chilly air.

Chapter 28

The Widow Watson sighed deeply as her lovely daughter-in-law, Annie, carefully tucked the quilt around her lap and placed the cup and saucer in her hands. The fragrant steam that drifted up from the hot tea was very soothing to the patient. She slowly sipped the hot brew.

"Thanks Honey," she said, swallowing carefully. "Mmmmm, that is so good. I'm so glad you and Max were able to come and stay with me for a while. I just don't know how I would've managed without you," her eyes became misty as she spoke. Annie was already accustomed to the emotions that were continually near the surface.

"Now, Mother Watson, you know we wouldn't want to be anywhere else right now. You just relax and enjoy your tea. Did you notice that I went out and put seed on the bird feeder? I already saw that big fat blue jay out there scolding the little chickadees," she said with a tender smile.

Widow Watson patted Annie's small hand and said, "I saw that, Annie, thank you. Now, Honey, you just go on about your business, and I'll be happy to sit here and watch my birds. I promise I'll be a good girl," she said with a sweet smile.

Annie gave her an affectionate squeeze and went across the room to the sewing corner where the Widow usually did the mending and other sewing for the community. She pulled the chair out and sat back down to continue on the skirt she was altering for one of Mother Watson's customers. I'm just glad that I can do something to really be of help to her. She is just about the dearest person I know, thought Annie. I felt so sorry for her when she couldn't go to Marie's funeral. Her injuries wouldn't allow it and it was not even here in

Madison. Her precious mother-in-law had cried and cried. She fought back tears of her own, as she prayed for Mother Watson.

***

Max was at the woodpile, splitting wood that wasn't entirely necessary, but it gave him something to do. There was a nice big stack near the shed that had been split by different ones in the community who either paid for sewing in that way, or stopped by to just be neighborly while the wife chatted with Mrs. Watson.

With each thrust of the axe, the man became more and more frustrated about the events that had caused them to be there. Not that he minded their coming, but he would have much rather come for other reasons than this.

He was so angry that someone would have the gall to cruelly beat up two defenseless old women. Why? Why? Why? Each time he slammed the axe into the wood, the word seemed to echo in his ears.

Thrusting the axe aside, he shoved his hands into his pockets and strode away from the woodpile. For a few minutes, he wandered aimlessly around the familiar farmyard, occasionally kicking at the snow dejectedly.

He and Annie had been here only a few days, and it was heartwarming to see his mother already well on the road to recovery from her physical ordeal. Losing her dearest friend in such a manner was going to take a lot longer to get over, he thought, but at least she is sleeping the night through again.

He shook his head and sighed as he recalled the first nights and her painful dreams and cries in the night. Annie would pray for Mother Watson, while Max gently held her in his arms. After a while, she would be able to sleep again. The love and prayers were helping her,

182

although Max was not quite ready to forgive God for allowing such a dreadful thing to happen. He was not even sure he could love God again. His faith had never truly reached true fullness as it had with Annie, and now he wasn't even sure he wanted to try. How could a loving God let this happen?

He absently stepped over to the cellar and pulled up the sloped wooden door, his mind suddenly alive with memories of childhood play...games of hide and seek and sliding down the cellar door after the first winter ice storm. He smiled a half-smile as he remembered his mother's warning about splinters. And then, he did smile as he remembered lying across her knees, thoroughly embarrassed as she gently picked them from his tender skin with the tweezers.

He went on down into the cellar, and stood, savoring the sweet odors there. Suddenly he was aware that the small light bulb was burning over the table. "That's odd," he said aloud, knowing that from long years of habit, his mother would never leave a light burning here.

He stepped over to turn it off and noticed the burlap bag on the table. Out of curiosity, he looked inside, finding hickory nuts, chestnuts and a canteen. There were also an axe head, some apples, a can of coffee, and a tube of toothpaste.

"Toothpaste?" He looked toward the door as though there might be a clue to this unusual item being in the root cellar.

So he took the bag and tossing it over his shoulder, he made his way up the steps, after turning off the light.

In a moment, Max was at the door, and just as he reached for the knob, it opened. He looked into his wife's sweet face, and they both spoke at once. "Hi!"

183

"Lunch is ready, Max. I was just about to call you," Annie said with a smile. He followed her into the house, putting the burlap bag on the floor of the enclosed porch. He kicked off his boots and hung his coat and hat on the coatrack beside the door. Quickly he washed up for the meal, and hurried to join them.

Annie had set up a little table out in the living room so that Mother Watson could eat with them. She sat there, waiting patiently for the two to settle themselves for the nice hot meal.

Annie folded her hands and said a brief prayer of thanks, and Max looked at both of them out of the corner of his eyes, as they prayed. Giving his head a little shake, as Annie said the amen, he reached for the coffee pot and poured their coffee. Annie ladled hot soup into their bowls and passed Mother Watson a napkin.

"Thank you, sweetheart. My, that soup smells good. I think I might just be able to eat this time," Mother Watson smoothed the napkin in her lap, and carefully placed the soup spoon to her mouth.

"Mm mm, that surely hits the spot, as your Daddy used to say," she said, smiling at Max. He agreed with her, taking a big bite of cornbread. They ate silently for a few minutes. Suddenly he spoke around a sweet pickle slice. "Say, Mom? Why on earth would you have toothpaste down in the root cellar?"

"What?" she answered in puzzlement, taking another bite. "Toothpaste? I don't know what you're talking about." She looked from Max to Annie, who shrugged her shoulders, as she wiped her mouth with her napkin.

"Why, Max? Did you find some down there??"

"Well, yeah, in a burlap bag with some other stuff. Chestnuts, apples, coffee, and... of all things... a canteen." He scratched the back of his head, and leaned

184

back holding the mug of coffee in his hand. "In fact, Mom, it reminded me of that old canteen I used to have years ago, now that I think of it!"

Now Mother Watson knew where the bag must have come from, and she hesitated to answer.

"Oh, and there was an axe head in the bag, too. It's out there in the porch. Do you want me to get it for you?" Max pushed his chair back and started to get up, but his mother put her hand on his arm and stopped him.

"That's all right, Maxie," she said. "Just relax and I'll tell you all about it."

And so, Mother Watson told the two all about the mysterious stranger who had been coming around for years trading with her and sometimes making repairs. She had felt a little sad at having the little secret told, as she had thoroughly enjoyed his comings and goings, along with the surprise of his gifts and the unexpected timing of his visits.

Max sat there quietly, letting her tell her whole story, incredulity seeming to come over him. She told of having seen the stranger a few times. "Just a glimpse, usually as he was leaving." Max was trying very hard to control his emotions, but his face was turning red and he worked the muscles on the sides of this jaws as she talked.

"Mom, don't you realize who you are talking about?" He deliberately spoke very quietly and as a result said each word slowly and distinctly, amazement accenting each syllable. He placed his hands flat on the table, and sat on the edge of his chair. As she shook her head while sipping the hot soup, he raised his bushy eyebrows in disbelief.

"Mother, he is *the killer!*" As the reality hit him, he did shove back his chair and stood to his stocking feet.

Moving to her side, he said, "Mother, he is the one who did this awful thing to you and Marie Jamison!"

"But, Maxie, that is just impossible. Why would a kind fellow like that ever want to hurt anyone?" Mother Watson put the napkin to her eyes, as the tears started to flow.

"Well, Mom, what did the stranger look like?" He asked her, more gently now.

"He was rather tall…well, very tall I would think. And it seems to me he had black hair and a beard, although I never really saw his face." She began to tremble, and Annie moved to put an afghan around her shoulders.

"Max? Maybe we should let her get back to bed for a rest just now," Annie turned to her husband with deep concern on her face.

"No, Annie! I must think," Mother Watson said, sniffing into the crumpled napkin. "The man who hit me and chased Marie…the one who was digging there in the woods…he had a black beard and hair. And Max," she said, dragging out his name in agony, and the tears started falling anew down her pale cheeks, "he was quite tall, too." She began to sob into her hands. They both went to her and comforted her until she was able to have another cup of tea.

And so, as Annie cleared away the remains of their lunch, Max told his mother all about the community meeting and the discovery that several folks in the area had seen the stranger. He told her about the carving identifying the man, and how it had been found at the site of the grave there in the woods. He told her about the robbery that apparently started the events that had so tragically affected his hometown.

Only the evening before, Old Jack had come by to see how they were getting along with the Widow

186

Watson, and he had filled Max in on the results of the search for the stolen loot. So now, Max told his mother the whole story and how they were at that very moment planning a trap that would catch the evil man and put a stop to all this once and for all.

Chapter 29

Larry was working in the grocery store that day with Mary Martin. Her husband Tom was taking his turn as a volunteer for the surveillance team that was spending twenty-four hours a day at the site of the shallow grave in the woods.

As Larry stocked shelves, and Mary swept the floor for the second time that morning, they were discussing the events of the last few days.

"Personally," Mary said, "I am so grateful to those people in the city for being willing to pay for an officer to watch the gravesite twenty-four hours a day. I'd hate for Tom to be out there with just volunteers and no deputy." She stopped and poised the broom on the toe of her shoe contemplating it with seeming interest.

She would be glad when his four-hour watch was over and he was safely back behind the counter of their little store. She heaved a deep sigh. "Larry, do you know who is watching with him this morning?"

She began to sweep again and made her way to the end of the aisle where he stooped to put bottles neatly on the shelf.

Straightening up, he said, "No, Mary, I'm not sure. I do know that Deputy Bill was out there last night with Bob Greyson. I think Bob had said that a deputy was coming over from Drayton to take Bill's place when his watch was over. I'm sure that this twenty-four hour watch is the right thing to do, though, don't you? After all, after so many times trying to find that map, the killer must not be willing to give up easily. The sheriff said that those people the loot was stolen from were terribly glad to get it back."

As it happened, they wouldn't actually take possession of the stolen goods until the whole matter was cleared up, but they were so relieved to know of its recovery that they offered to help finance a surveillance team to trap the killer.

The sheriff had notified proper authorities of its location, and the couple who owned the property came over to Madison personally to identify the contents of the crate that had been found in the woods. Everything was meticulously packed in newspaper inside the crate that had been carefully wrapped with heavy plastic and securely taped with a heavy cloth tape.

There were priceless family heirlooms, lovely antique jewels that had been in the wealthy family for generations. There was also a leather zipper bag with quite a large number of new bills inside. And of course, there was all the family silver and some very expensive cut-glass pieces that the couple was especially thrilled about having recovered. They were gifts from a deceased daughter and had tremendous sentimental value. People were not surprised to learn that the value of the contents of the crate was over ninety thousand dollars in all.

The members of the search party had stood wide-eyed, almost reverently that day in the city hall where the crate had been officially opened. They were mutually stunned at the beauty and value of the items that they'd all had a hand in recovering.

And to think…this is why so many have been killed and hurt. Just unbelievable, Bob Greyson stood with his cap in his hands, shaking his head in disbelief.

The entire group had dispersed solemnly and silently that morning, each with their own grim thoughts. No one could believe all that had happened.

Each man had volunteered to help keep watch over the gravesite and would be notified when their four-hour watch would take place. Each and every one of them had a prayer in their hearts that the twenty-four hour watch would not have to last for long. They all wanted an end to this misery.

Larry put the last item on the shelf and stood up dusting his hands on the white apron he wore. He began to gather the empty boxes from around him, as Mary propped the broom near the large old pot-bellied stove.

"How about a cup of coffee and a break, Larry?" she said as she took their mugs from a shelf near the stove.

"Oh, thanks, Mary," he said, taking the steaming mug and folding his lanky frame onto a wooden nail keg that was there. "I'm glad the weather has cleared up some," he said, gazing out the window nearby. He lapsed into silence, and somehow, Mary knew something was bothering him.

She sat quietly on the tall stool next to the counter and sipped the hot soothing liquid.

"Mary?" Larry swiveled on the keg to face her. "Did you know that Jill had been sick for a while before she…well, before she disappeared?" He stared into the cup absently.

"Yes, Larry, I guess her mother mentioned that during the search. Said she hadn't been feeling too good. Why? Was it anything serious?" Mary looked over her coffee cup at him, with a puzzled frown.

"Oh, I guess not. Mother invited Joan and Frank over for supper last night and somehow, we all got to talking about Jill. You know my sister Linda has always been weak and sickly. Well, I guess her struggling with a bout of asthma last night kinda got Jill's parents to remembering about Jill's being sick. I really never knew what was wrong with her until last night, but I did know that she hadn't felt well. They said that she'd been in to the doctor the day before… the hayride… and had had some blood tests done. The results didn't come back

190

until she was... already gone," Larry's eyes misted, and he sighed deeply.

"Larry, what was wrong with her?" Mary asked compassionately of her young friend.

"Oh," he said, straightening his shoulders, and taking a long drink of coffee. "It was some kind of anemia with a big long name. Seems she only had some deficiencies that needed taking care of." He paused, thinking of all they had said the night before.

'It's kinda funny 'cause they said that the doctor first thought it was leukemia," the young man swallowed past a lump in his throat.

"I still can't get used to her being...gone, Mary. It hurts so bad to know I'll never see her again," Larry lowered his head and stared at the floor between his knees.

"I know," she said sympathetically. "It's the same for Tom and me, and Wilma, too. I'm so glad you've been coming to pray with us each morning before work. We all just knew it would help you like it has us."

"Well, Mary, it sure has, and last night I told Frank and Joan about our prayer times. I invited them to come and pray with us sometime...I hope that was okay with you and Tom." Larry raised his eyebrows questioningly as he turned and looked at her.

"Oh yes Larry! That would be wonderful! I know they hurt as badly as Tom and I. Losing their daughter was so painful for them," the tears began to sting behind her eyes as she spoke.

"How is your sister Linda getting along? Does she have those asthma attacks very often?" Mary could see tears in Larry's brown eyes, too, and decided to change the subject.

"Not as often as she did for a while, though..." Larry stopped in mid-sentence as a rather loud commotion at the door drew their attention. It was Bones Jones, "making his appearance" as Mary would call it. Larry smiled at the thought as he stood and sat his cup back up on the shelf.

"Howdy, Bones. Care for a cup of coffee? Help yourself, I've already loafed off too much," he said to Mary with a wink.

Mary let out a sigh of relief, as she saw the improvement in Larry's mood. Everyone usually got a kick out of Bone's odd ways and manners, and yet, she felt a familiar sense of dread at having that hard-hearted man come into the store these days. He usually managed to stop at least once or twice every day since the town meeting just recently.

"Well, Miss Mary, any news?" he spoke loudly and quite sarcastically, his small head bobbing on top of that long neck.

"No, not really, Bones," she said, making herself busy behind the counter.

"They still got spies out watching for that 'mountain man'? I keep telling everyone, they ain't gonna catch him thataway," Bones settled himself on the keg that Larry had just left.

"I know Bones," she said softly, without looking up from wiping the already shining counter.

Larry had moved to the far side of the small store and started straightening items on the top shelves. He could just see the top of Bones' raggedy old hat bobbing up and down as he talked. He could visualize the shifty eyes and long pointed nose, wrinkling with expression.

"Seems to me, they coulda handled the whole thing a lot better," he said, leaning his tall skinny back up against the wall and propping one long thin elbow up on a low shelf.

192

Oh, what is he going to start in on, this time, Lord? Mary thought to herself. Father God, give me patience to deal with this man. It gets harder and harder to have him come here.

"…and those little red shirts," Bones was saying with emphasis.

Mary's heart leapt within her as she realized the reference to her darling twin boys.

"What?" she said, as her hand fluttered to her throat.

"Hey, Bones, can you give me a hand over here?"

As Bones moved toward Larry's call, the telephone rang, and Mary was so thankful for the interruption. By the time she was finished with her conversation, several customers had come into the store, and she was continually busy with them until Tom returned from his watch in the woods.

Chapter 30

It was late in the evening and Jill sat very near the fireplace, enjoying both its warmth and the light it had provided for reading. She gently laid the Bible down in her lap and began to slowly rock the small chair in which she sat.

She reached down to the hearth beside her and picked up the steaming cup of rosehip tea that Andy had given her before he went out. As she savored the distinctive aroma of the vitamin C-rich tea, she remembered his exuberance the day he came in with a pail of rosehips swinging from his thick arm. She slowly sipped the savory brew, smiling at the memory.

"Well, here ya are, Punkin'," he had said with a smile as he moved to the corner fireplace. There was a big black kettle snuggled against the coals for a continual supply of hot water. There were two bunks head to head in the opposite corner that were now made up with Andrew's blankets and animal hides. The old, worn, hand-made table was the centerpiece of the room, with the small rocker and its table between the window and the fireplace.

Andy had stooped his mighty frame, and taking up the large kettle, he poured the steaming water into the small tea kettle they had found on the top shelf to the left of the fireplace. As he tossed in a big handful of the dried rosehips, he chattered gaily to his young friend.

"Little One, this will have you fixed up in no time," he had said with a wink.

"Did you know a small kettle like this, made with a handful of these will make a cup of tea with as much vitamin C as more than a dozen oranges? Yep, I read all about it in one of my newspapers. Did you know you can make rosehip jelly out of these, too?" Shaking his head, he continued, "Too bad we don't have sugar or we would make some!"

Jill smiled now, as she sipped the tea he had made so devotedly for her for days now. She thought lovingly of all the little things he continually found to do to make her comfortable and to try and strengthen her. Each time he came in with fresh small game for a meal, he made sure that she ate the cooked liver. He told her determinedly how it was by far the tastiest bit of meat to be found and assured her of the tremendous good it would do her.

She did not have the heart to tell him that she had always detested liver, and that, in fact, she rarely ate meat at all. She did not care for its taste or texture. She could remember having had stomach flu or some such ailment when she was a child, and after having eaten a large portion of roast beef and promptly losing it, she could never quite enjoy meat. So, as a result, she always made it a choice to avoid the distasteful reminder of "that time when she was so sick".

She thought now of the fried squirrel meat that they had had for supper and the fact that she had eaten the whole tiny liver... just for him. Oddly enough, it seemed she was actually beginning to like the odd flavored meat.

She smiled again and got up from the small rocking chair and put more wood on the fire. She noticed it was quite dark outside and moved over to the shiny lamp on the wall bracket. She would light it for Uncle Andy as he would be coming in soon from taking care of the horse. They were careful to use the precious oil sparingly, as all they had were the three small cans they had found in the shed.

Standing there, she slowly traced her finger along the neat block letters that had been burned into the log wall below the lamp. "May the good Lord bless all who may take refuge in this here cabin." There underneath was the burnt-in signature "Abe", with the Bible verse, Deuteronomy 33:27.

Jill remembered going to the worn Bible that "Abe" had left for them. Gently turning the pages, she had looked up that verse and now had it memorized. It was carefully underlined; "The eternal God is thy refuge, and underneath are the everlasting arms:"

That overwhelming feeling of peace stole over her as it had that first night. To know that God had a message of reassurance for them at the end of their long journey had truly touched both their hearts. They had prayed their thanks together that night and every night since. They were spending lots of hours reading the Bible together. First one, then the other read aloud at the table or before the cozy fire.

They also spent much time speculating about their unknown friend, Abe. Was he a type like Abe Lincoln, tall and quiet and gentle? Or what about Father Abraham of the Bible? They had gone there and read all about that wondrous old man of God. Then Jill thought perhaps he was a Benjamin Franklin type with a bald head and slightly long hair all around. This one, she had said with a giggle, would be chubby, with clean-shaven rosy cheeks, and shiny spectacles sliding down his nose. Any of the three "Abes" were delightfully lovable and most dear to the hearts of the two who had taken refuge in that small cabin.

***

At length, Andrew came into the cabin, shaking the snow from his feet and hanging up his coat and hat on the pegs behind the door.

196

"Did you spend some time at the grave, Uncle Andy?" Jill asked with concern in her blue eyes.

"Yes, Little Jill, I did. And you know what? It gets easier every time I go out there. What a friend we have in our Abe who buried my two friends for me." Andy stooped beside the fire to give it a good stirring and pour himself another cup of the rosehip tea.

Sitting down at the table beside Jill, they were quietly enjoying one another, with only the occasional crackling and popping of the burning wood to break the silence. Both found their thoughts going back to the day they had arrived here and how Andy had discovered the wooden cross he had made years before. It was situated near the remaining old pine tree, and it was obvious that someone had placed it there for a grave marker. Someone had burned small letters into the crosspiece, "Rest in Peace". Somehow, Andrew knew it was the final resting place for Peter and Billy, who had died in the fire so many years before.

"Abe sure fixed up a nice place here, didn't he?" Jill said over the top of her cup of tea. Her smile warmed his heart, as usual.

"Yes, he surely did! It seems like it was just made to order for our needs, too, don't you think? Like the little corral and shed so handy for Ebony, and lots of firewood ready to hand?"

Jill chuckled, "That sounds just like Honest Abe, to do such a thing as leaving plenty of firewood. And I can just imagine the ancient patriarch Abraham gently currying a horse in that little shed…" Jill gazed into the fire with a pleasant light in her eyes. "And then there's Abe 'Franklin' who left the Bible and the messages right from the heart of God just for us!" She shifted her gaze to the face of her beloved friend, who responded with a hearty affectionate laugh.

197

"Jill, I am so glad the Lord brought us together! You make life such fun!" He reached over and rumpled her hair and got up from the table. He began to close the shutters on the windows while she banked the fire for the night. The cold outside seemed far away within the snug little cabin.

As Jill moved about with nightly tasks, she felt the gratitude of her heart swelling up until she found a lump in her throat. She knew that prayer time tonight would be even more special than usual, and yet, somewhere in the deep recesses of her mind was a growing uneasiness that she could not begin to put into words. There was a sense of something that she could not yet explain.

Chapter 31

Sheriff Billings sat on the steps in the sunshine with his hands supporting his chin. Bob Greyson came out of the cabin with two mugs of steaming coffee and sat beside the man who had come to be a frequent visitor at the Greysons' home.

"Thanks, Bob," the sheriff said, taking the mug gratefully. "This whole thing is starting to get to me, if you know what I mean."

Bob nodded his head in agreement and clapped a hand on his friend's shoulder sympathetically. "Yeah, it has been a big disappointment not finding the killer's hiding place. But, you know, it could just be all that fresh snow we had about the time we started looking."

"Well, it's plain the killer isn't using any hideout up there now, or else we'd a seen tracks for sure!" The sheriff sipped the hot coffee gingerly, so as not to burn his lips, and absently scratched behind Husky's ears. The big faithful dog sat at his feet.

"One thing that *is* reassuring is the fact that we got such clear prints from your crowbar, Bob. When we do catch this crazy man, there's no way he will get away with the grief he's caused all our people," the sheriff stated emphatically, as he rubbed the back of his weary neck.

"He just might as well plan on spending the rest of his life in prison. Personally, I hope they give him the death sentence!" He cupped his coffee mug in his hands and stared off in the distance.

Bob looked at the sheriff with compassion in his eyes. "Yes, he probably does deserve that and more, but, well, we really ought to be praying for him. He must have had some rotten life to drive him to do all that he has done."

199

"Oh, yeah, I'll pray for him, but I still don't want him running loose ever again, rotten life, or no rotten life!"

"Sheriff," Bob began, choosing his words carefully. "Do you remember the other night when I had watch with the twins' daddy, Tom?"

"Sure, the night that Officer Paulson was here, right? Why?" The sheriff sat his empty mug down on the step beside him and put his elbows on his knees, clasping his big hands. He stared at his scuffed boots.

"That night Tom told me some amazing things about his family. Remember what a tough time Wilma had after the twins' death? Well, somewhere along in there, Tom and Mary and Wilma began to have special prayer times for the one who had killed the boys. He said they could not understand how or why it had happened, or even how they would ever overcome it." He swallowed past a lump in his throat. "But do you know what they asked God to do? They asked him to use the situation to His Glory." Bob idly traced his finger around the rim of his coffee cup. He took a deep breath and his friend sat silently waiting for him to continue.

"He said that they consciously prayed every day, sometimes many times each day for their boys' killer, whoever he was. And then, Tom said they'd asked Larry to come pray with them. He has hurt so bad since Jill was killed. So he's been praying with them every day."

Bob took another deep breath, swallowed again, and looked at the sheriff. "And then what he told me really gets to me, Sheriff. He said that you can't pray for someone that often, whoever he is, without beginning to love and care about him. Can you imagine that?" He gazed at the older Christian man in wonder.

The sheriff shook his head and took off the cap he wore. "I surely can't, Bob. Must be something like a miracle, I guess. What else did he say about their feelings?"

"For one thing, they are beginning to believe that there is some kind of divine purpose in all this. They are praying for the man to find the saving knowledge of Christ!"

"That's awesome, Bob! But, don't they believe that he ought to be punished for what he's done?" The sheriff asked incredulously.

"Oh, of course! But they know that with God in his life and Christ as Lord of his life, then his time of punishment won't be a waste. He will be able to accept the punishment and whatever his life brings, through the grace of God. And who knows, maybe he would even lead others to Christ right there in prison!"

As Bob talked, he stood up and paced a few steps back and forth on the packed snowy path. "Do you know what else they have all done, sheriff?" He stopped and thrusting his hands deep in the pockets of his coat, he looked deeply into the eyes of his friend. "They have completely forgiven this killer," he said softly, reverently, with a slight shake of his head. "I wish I would have that kind of faith, don't you?"

There was a rustling sound at the corner of the cabin where the path went around to the woodpile. Bob looked at the sheriff with a wrinkled brow and moved to see who had been there. He saw Randy quietly sobbing into his hands there beside the woodpile, the armload of wood he had carried lay forgotten at his feet.

When Randy realized his daddy was beside him, he sobbed all the harder and looking up at him with anguish on his young face, he cried, "Daddy, how could they? How could they forgive a murderer?" He sniffed and wiped his nose with the back of his hand. "Don't they love Kenny and Kelly anymore? Oh, Daddy, they

201

were my best friends," he said, sobbing so hard that it broke Bob's heart.

But then, Randy allowed his daddy to wrap his loving arms around and hold him until the tears ceased many minutes later. Bob prayed silently as he held his son. God, what do I say to him? Could I have forgiven someone for taking his life like Tom and Mary did? Like Wilma did? Could I? Bob searched his own heart and sought the will of his Heavenly Father, as the tears silently poured down his own face.

***

Susan Greyson came out on the porch with the large porcelain percolator in her hands.

"More coffee, anyone?" she said, as she turned to pull the door shut behind her.

"Oh, where is Bob? I thought he was out here with you, Sheriff." Susan moved to pour coffee into the mug he had picked up from the steps and held out to her, as he stood on the bottom step.

"Aww, Susan, he and Randy are back there… talking. We'd just been discussing his conversation with Tom about his family's reaction to all of this when Randy came long. I guess he heard something that upset him, because when I looked, he was crying and they seemed to be having a 'heart to heart' talk back there."

"Poor Randy," his mother said pitifully. "All this has been awfully hard on him. And Bob told me about the Martins' forgiving the killer. It is truly beyond me, and I just imagine that it is terribly hard for Randy. Unforgiveness is a difficult thing to conquer. But you know, Sheriff, I've been doing a lot of seeking and praying about this myself, and after all, we who are in Christ Jesus are conquerors through Him, aren't we? Well, I have been truly asking God to give me love and forgiveness for this killer. I'm not sure I have it just yet, but at least I am beginning to feel a sense of peace for the first time since all of this started."

"Oh, yeah? Well, I could use some of that about now myself," and with that, the weary man sunk again to the steps where he had been sitting earlier. He absently wiped at the coffee he'd sloshed from his cup onto the porch.

Susan took a step toward him desiring to bring him some kind of reassurance, when she heard the insistent ring of the telephone inside. She knew that her daughter June was in the shower, so she excused herself and rushed to answer the phone.

In just a moment, she was back at the door. "Sheriff? It's for you! Sounds real important!"

The uniformed man hurried into the cabin and quickly took the phone from the countertop where it lay.

"Billings here... Yeah? When? Ya don't say! Great! I'll be right there!"

He slammed the receiver back onto the phone and with a mixture of awe and delight, he declared with the blood rushing to his face, "They've got him! They caught the killer!

"Tell Bob that I'll call later, will ya?" And pushing his cap firmly on his head, he rushed out the door, forgetting to close it in his haste.

Stunned, Susan followed him to the door and stood in the doorway watching his official car as it sped away. Bob came around from the back of the house.

"Where is he going in such a hurry?" He stood there, scratching his head, and turned to Susan. She still stood in the doorway, white around the lips and beginning to tremble. With eyes dark and wide, she said in a very small voice, "They caught the killer, Bob."

Chapter 32

That very morning before dawn a man drove down the country roads near Madison. His hands tightly gripped the steering wheel until the knuckles were white.

He was feeling quite optimistic about it all. For one thing, the car he had "borrowed" had a full tank of gas, and he had no concern about having that problem again! Plus, it was not snowing this morning so that would make his task easier and the driving much more effective.

Within just a few minutes, he would have the map he had tried for so long to get, and then he could retreat until springtime and come and recover the loot that was rightfully his, after all. Then he would take his sister and leave this country for good and put all this unpleasant life behind him.

It was never to have gone this far, he thought. The three old school buddies were going to do this one job, his first and supposedly their last. They had insisted that if he would do "just this one job" with them, he would be set for life and they would give up their lives of crime in gratitude for his cooperation. He had never felt fully convinced of their intentions, but his desperation made him receptive to their comradeship and promises.

After all, his sister was the real reason he got into this mess, as it was her constant complaining of their meager existence that caused him to respond when Henry and Jake first approached him. Oh, he truly felt sorry for her, and loved her because she was his sister after all. But he would never forgive their parents for dying and leaving the badly crippled girl in his care. He worked many long hours as dishwasher in the hotel restaurant and provided the best he knew how for her needs. She had been in a wheelchair for as many years as he could remember, although there were menial things she could do around their tiny apartment. She was able to care for most of her personal needs, although he tired immensely of washing her hair week after week.

Now he harbored dreams of having money to hire a companion for her. Someone who could help her around the little house he hoped to get one day. There would be a white picket fence and flowers along the pathway. That would make her so happy, he thought. She is only such a grouch because she is forced to live like a hermit in that dingy little apartment. Her companion would be a very nice little lady who would read her stories and work puzzles with her. Her one pleasure, it seemed, were the few large jigsaw puzzles he had been able to acquire over the years. She always had one set up on the card table partly done. When all of this was over, he would see to it that she had all the puzzles she ever wanted and someone to be with her and be her friend.

"It could have all been over by now if that Jake would've been straight with me," he mumbled, as he neared the outskirts of Madison. He remembered that day when he and Jake had gone to look for the loot. He had been stunned when Jake told him that Henry had been killed in an accident at the saw mill. He said that Henry had given some vague directions as to where he had buried the loot… near the river by lower Madison.

They had looked and looked that morning early in the fall. He remembered his growing confusion and anger at Jake's edgy attitude and the way it seemed that Jake was getting less and less sure of where the loot was.

Had he known Jake's thoughts that morning, he would not have been surprised to know that Jake had come to realize that without Henry, they only had to divide the loot two ways, then recognized that *without Ray*, he could have it all to himself! He'd been rebuking himself for bringing Ray out here at all, when he could have just come quietly and disappeared with all the money! He had come out that morning determined to do whatever it took to get Raymond Jay out of the picture, and had not even thought of that easy solution. Now, Jake was angry at himself and at Ray.

The two men found themselves on edge and so easily angered that before long, Jake said one too many hard things to Ray. Ray had lashed out at him, swinging backhanded at the side of Jake's head, and he tumbled over a dead tree and down a ravine that was there. Ray knew in an instant that Jake was hurt extremely bad. Something in the way he twisted his neck at the bottom of the ravine made Ray's stomach turn. He lurched over the fallen tree and scrambled down to his partner. Somehow, he knew this was a fatal thing. Jake murmured something with grotesque hatred in his eyes.

"What did you say? Gee, I'm awful sorry, Jake. I never meant…" But he never finished the sentence as Jake repeated himself.

"You will never find it… *never…*" and he was gone. He died right there near the river, to Ray's dismay.

Ray shuddered now, as he recalled the look in Jake's dying eyes. He had knelt there, stunned by the man's words and trying to grasp what had happened.

Suddenly, he had become aware of someone nearby. He turned and then had seen the double vision. Twin boys in red flannel shirts were there watching him, each with a fishing pole in one hand.

He shook his head determinedly now, to remove the memory from him. He did not want to recall those next two dreadful hours when he hastily buried the body with the two wide-eyed boys tied nearby. He did not want to recall how he had "done away" with them in his panic stricken haste to get away. Or how he had stupidly

206

taken their fishing poles with him so that there would be no evidence found, or how he had sneaked back a day or two later and put them beside the river, thinking that someone would find them and assume the boys had drowned accidentally.

He had tried for weeks to sleep and could never get any of this out of his mind. Then, one night in bed, he lay staring into the darkness. Suddenly, he realized that Jake must have had a map! How else could he have been so sure that he, Raymond Jay Peters, would never find the loot? Astonished at this thought, he had sat up straight in the bed with his hands pushing on the sides of his face. After all, he deserved it. He had not gone through all this for nothing. Plus, both robbery partners were dead, and he had read in the paper that he, the third partner, had never been identified. And with the only two witnesses dead, he reasoned…again shuddering down to the pit of his stomach… he should be able to go back, easily dig up the body and get the map.

He had tried twice to do this, but surely, being cold and bitter weather now, there would be no little girl out horseback riding, or two old ladies taking a walk.

***

"Grand Central Station, that's what it is," he murmured. Firmly gripping the steering wheel, he sat straighter in the car seat and prepared to get himself mentally ready for the task ahead. He recalled the distaste he had experienced when he had been digging the last two times. Both times, he had felt that awful sickness deep within, as his hands sought the presence of the body beneath the earth.

He took some relief in the thought that perhaps now the body would be thoroughly frozen in the shallow grave. Yes, that would make the whole thing much easier, he thought, as he parked the car. It will be just like going through the pockets of a dummy at the department store. He smiled at the thought.

"This may be much easier than I expected", he said aloud, gaining confidence now as he began the walk into the snow covered woods.

It was just at twilight. The sky was beginning to lighten and each star was fading from the night sky as day came stealing across.

Ray's breath came in frosty clouds before him, causing quick icicles to form on his bushy black beard. He reached up to rub them away and felt that tender prickle of the scar tissue on his face. He was so accustomed to the feeling he hardly noticed it any more. It had taken years for him to overcome the trauma that he had experienced when the propane bottle exploded, burning his face and temporarily blinding him. He had been a youngster then, playing with other boys in the garbage dumpster behind the dingy apartment building where they lived. His dad was already dead at the time, and it had been only he and his mother and the older sister in the wheelchair. They tried to help him as much as possible as he went through long, long nights filled with nightmares and excruciating pain.

That was all like a bad dream now and only flashed into his mind in a fraction of a second, as he wiped the frost from his scraggly mustache.

It didn't take very long to find the path he had taken before. It was snow covered and obviously in disuse. Good, he thought, this means no interruptions this time. He hurried his step and keeping alert for the landmark that told him where to leave the path, he wished for the crowbar he had had last time he was here.

Maybe it is still there at the grave, he thought, although he hadn't much hopes of finding it in all the deep snow.

He remembered how he had come to have that handy tool, taken from that same shed where he had found the can of gasoline. But, for some reason, he just could not remember when he had last seen it. Oh, well, at least it saved me from getting chewed up by that wolf-dog, he thought with a wry smile.

He recalled his frustration at not being able to catch the swift little pony that Christmas Day. He refused to let any thought of the little girl creep into his mind. That was the absolute worst thing that had come out of this whole affair.

He had gone into the shed he had found and was hopefully looking for some gasoline to take back to the car he thought he would have to abandon. He had been so angry, and had strewn the shed with whatever he could grab.

Kicking a lantern over as he left the shed, he triumphantly held a full can of gasoline in his hand. He stepped out of the shed door, and as he did, a very large dog stepped around the corner of the cabin there. It would have been hard to guess who was more startled, but the dog began barking fiercely and biting at the man's legs. He knew the man was an intruder.

"Stop that! Stop it!" the man demanded, grabbing a crowbar from where it hung on the outside wall of the shed. He wanted to run, but the dog circled him, barking and snarling, trying to bite his leg.

"I said *stop*!" He shouted, and the big man brought the crowbar down hard on the back of the dog's neck. The large animal collapsed into a heap and Ray hurried away, taking the gas can and crowbar along.

***

Soon he came to the place where he could leave the path, and again his mind was alive with memories. This was the spot where the two women had watched him and he had to stop them from being able to identify him. He had watched the papers and never heard what they had told, so he assumed they were both dead. Why did they have to be so nosey, he thought. He remembered how bad he had felt when the skinny old lady had died there beside the root cellar. And then there was that stupid man coming out of the cellar. I fixed him good, I guess, he thought grimly.

He could not get over how little he had been able to find in the Drayton paper about what had been happening in Madison. That suits me fine, he thought, nervously looking around as he hurried into the woods. There were no tracks anywhere to be seen, and there was ample light now, as the sun just touched the horizon through the forest of stark and barren trees.

He had no trouble finding the spot. After all, I've been here often enough, he thought bitterly. He began rapidly to scoop the snow away from the gravesite, using a small spade he had brought. He would use the sharp digging point to chisel away the frozen soil and hopefully finish with this dreaded task and be home long before noon.

So intense was he at his work that he had no awareness that he was not alone. Suddenly, out of the silence of the frosty morning air, he heard a gruff voice.

"Sorry fella, but you're not gonna find anything there."

Raymond J. Peters blinked twice, tried to swallow with a mouth gone intensely dry, and without moving anything but his head, he looked up. Right into the muzzle of a twelve gauge shotgun held firmly by the officer that stood there. He was vaguely aware that there

210

were other men there, but his mind refused to react. He
was absolutely numb.

Chapter 33

The next afternoon, Max Watson came into Madison for a few items needed at the store and found a small crowd gathered on the front driveway near the gas pumps.

"Hey, Max! Didja hear?" It was Bones Jones, grating on everyone's nerves as always. "We done caught us that there killer," he stated importantly to the bewildered man.

"Whaddya mean, *we?*" A man who stood there protested indignantly.

Ignoring him, Bones hurried over to the newcomer so that he could be the first to tell him the news. "You say they caught the killer? I don't believe it; that's great news! When did this happen?" Max was clearly amazed.

Bones knew he had himself a captive audience now, so he proceeded to repeat the news he had only heard a few minutes ago himself. He threw his arm over Max's shoulder and steered him away from the group, talking rapidly and expressively, waving his other arm all about.

Bob Greyson shook his head in wonder at the boldness of the man. He said to Tom, "It is a big relief to know that all this trauma can finally come to an end, isn't it, Tom?"

"Yes, it sure is, Bob. We've all waited so long for this day and it is hard to believe that the killer has already been taken to the city for arraignment and trial. I didn't see the man, although I understand he fit the description and the fingerprints on your crowbar. I guess he made a full confession, as well, although a few things are not quite clear just yet." He stopped talking and seemed to be lost in thought for a moment, and then, he thrust his hands into his pockets and looked at Bob earnestly.

"One thing sorta worries me, Bob. They said he was going on about a crippled sister that depends on him, and how he can't afford to be away from her. Isn't that strange?" He pulled the collar of his coat up around his ears against the wind and finished filling Bob's gas tank for him.

"Oh, thanks, Tom! I could have done that!" Bob protested, while screwing in the gas cap as Tom replaced the hose.

"Come on in. I'll buy you a cup of coffee," Tom said to Bob as he crossed his arms and briskly slapped his hands against his shoulders as they went inside to get out of the cold. "See you fellas later," he said from the door with a wave of his hand to the others who had gathered.

Bob followed him inside the store and the others drifted away, talking quietly with one another. All except Max and Bones who had sat inside the cab of Bones' pickup with the doors open. Bones was agitating Max into quite a state with his talk of hate and revenge and "what's right is right" and "they oughta hang that dirty dog!"

As the two men swept in with the cold air close on their heels, Larry pointed out to them that it looked like Bones was making quite a fuss out there. With much concern, they looked through the window and saw both men in heated discussion with angry emotion on their faces.

"You don't suppose that is good for Max, do ya, what with his mother being hurt and all?" Larry raised his eyebrows as he put the question to the two men who peered out the window with him.

"Nope!" Tom said emphatically. He went back to the door and jerked it open. "Hey, Max, come on in where it's warm, why don'tcha? I'll buy you a cup of coffee. You too, Bones," he called amiably.

"Aww, you go on ahead, I gotta get home anyhow," Bones said disappointedly and closed his door as Max got out of the truck. "See ya around, Max," he said with a scowl. They could hear him talking to himself as he drove slowly away.

Max ducked his head against the wind, which seemed to be colder and stronger now than it was a little bit ago. He hurried into the little store, checking his inside pocket to make sure the list Annie had sent was still there.

"Well, I'm glad I was still here when they caught that dirty dog," Max stated flatly, using one of Bones' names. "With any luck they will give him the chair! Right, Tom? I guess you're the gladdest one of us all outside of Jill's folks and the doc."

Max moved to the side of the potbellied stove and gratefully took the cup of coffee that was handed to him. Bob and Tom glanced at one another with barely perceptible shakes of their heads. This was going to be difficult. Mary was behind the counter and found herself beginning to pray. She reached out and patted Larry's arm as he went by, headed for the back room.

***

Meanwhile, in a dark, dingy little apartment in Drayton, a middle aged woman in a wheelchair was weeping. Bitter tears of self-pity coursed down her lined haggard face. "Alone, alone," she muttered over and over through her tears. Occasionally she found herself wracked with deep painful sobbing.

She blew hard into the saturated handkerchief she had clutched in her fingers. Pushing her chair nearer to the window, she peered up at the pale winter sky above the building next door.

"Don't know why that Raymond Jay had to go and git his self into such a mess. Now I'll be stuck in some institution somewhere, and he will rot in jail," she said to the dirty glass window. "Raymond Jay, you've been good to me, even if I ain't been the nicest person," she sobbed into the hanky again.

Presently, she continued talking as if her brother were there to hear. "I jest can't believe you went and kilt someone and that atryin' to get money so's we could have a little house with a picket fence. I love you, Raymond Jay...ohhh..." she wailed. "I *hate* you Raymond Jay Peters, for doin' this to us!"

Maybelle Peters buried her face in her hands and cried out her grief. She knew they would be coming for her sometime in the next few hours, and she did not want to go anywhere! She only wanted Raymond Jay to come home like he always had. He had told her she would be taken care of, that someone from the county welfare would be there to help her. She heard the pain in his voice as he had said that.

She knew it was something he would have never wanted; to be a "welfare case". He had always taken pride in the fact that he brought in whatever meager income they had by the hard work of his own two hands.

"Dishwater hands!" She virtually screamed the words in her frustration.

Violently shoving her chair backward from the window and maneuvering around the arm chair, she grabbed pillows and magazines from the couch and end table and clumsily threw them across the room.

"All you ever could do was wash someone else's dirty dishes! You rotten good for nothing! How could you leave me all alone?"

Wearily, she stopped near the card table where her latest jigsaw puzzle lay partly done.

"Why, oh why, Raymond Jay?" She laid her head on her crossed arms and wept until she was spent.

In a bit, she picked up the television control and absently pushed the "on" button, sniffing and wiping her eyes with the soggy hanky.

"You are not alone, my friend. God loves you!" The words pierced deeply into her heart, and she gazed at the television in amazement. There stood a man, a so-called TV evangelist, and he was pointing his finger right at her!

"My friend," the man said gently, "no matter what your problems, or where you may be, you need never feel alone again. You see, God is merciful and loving, and He sent His only Son to earth. And do you know why? To die. Just for you!"

Everything seemed so strange to Maybelle. The man seemed to look right into her eyes.

"He died so that you might have everlasting life with Him. And everlasting life starts right now, this very minute. Scripture says, 'Today is the day of salvation', my friend, so don't wait another minute. You can accept Jesus Christ the only Son of the Living God. The One and only God who created all! If you will take His Son and let Him cleanse you, He will forgive you of all your sins to be remembered no more! Never! Salvation is a gift, but you must receive it," the preacher said earnestly. "Then, starting right this very minute, He will be with you every day for the rest of your life here on this hearth. And what's more, He will take you into His loving arms for all eternity! Make Jesus Christ Lord of your life now. Give yourself to Him. He is the answer! 'He is the Way, the Truth, and the Life' and He said that no one could get to God, the Father, except through Him. Won't you come to Jesus today? He will take away all your heartache and pain. He will be your strength, and you will always be

216

able to lean on Him. He will be with you no matter what life brings your way. You see, He truly loves you, my friend."

Tears were flowing again, down Maybelle's face. She had said the prayer with the preacher, and she sat quietly now. There was a sense of Peace flooding over her, and yet, she did not quite know why. "Jesus, Jesus, Jesus," her very soul seemed to cry out His Name.

Chapter 34

Far away, a few weeks later, the huge man stood on the hill overlooking the little cabin site with its single lone pine tree. He drew deep strong breaths of the clean mountain air and gave praise to the God he had known for these few short months. In that snug log cabin below was the child of his heart.

He felt a tiny inner twinge of anguish deep inside, knowing she would not live long, but the peace of God stole over him, as it had done again and again. He knew, but for her coming into his life, he would have never come to know his Lord and Savior, Jesus Christ. "I truly believe she is an angel sent just to lead me to You, Jesus," the giant of a man said softly, as he swallowed a lump in his throat.

"Even if she will be here just a short time, I thank You for what You've done through her. And, Father, I thank You that she has been feeling so much better these days. At least she is not suffering or so very ill as she was just before we came here. Thank You, Lord Jesus, for our friend Abe, too," Andrew said with a big smile as he gazed fondly down at the tiny cabin with its soft curl of smoke rising from the chimney.

"Thank You for having him to give a decent burial to my friends, and for building this warm little cabin. And, Father, how I thank You for the bountiful supply of food he left here."

The big man smiled again, and looking down at his hands resting on his ample front, he chuckled. Then, looking for off into the sky and watching the towering white cloud that moved there, he said, "Father, most of all, I want to thank You for having Abe leave a Bible here for us. You just don't know what a strength it has been to both of us."

Then, shuffling his big foot in the snow, he grinned sheepishly, "Well, of course You know that! After all, You know everything!"

Andy picked up the two rabbits he had snared and moved swiftly down the hillside. In just a few minutes, he was inside the cabin, stomping the snow from his boots.

"It's getting mighty warm out there, Little One. Hey, you won't be so little for long if you keep eatin' like that," he said heartily, with a big smile, as he put the rabbits in a large pot there.

She smiled with her mouth full and the spoon poised in the air. Swallowing, she said, "But Uncle, you said you were glad I was showing some appetite again!" With a big grin, she wiped her mouth with a cloth.

"Well, yeah, but you'll get plumb fat eating all that blackstrap molasses, my dear," he said playfully.

"At least we don't have to worry about running out, Uncle. Can you imagine anyone having two whole gallons of blackstrap molasses?" She raised her eyebrows at him as she took another big mouthful of the granola soaked with the sticky syrup.

"We better have a lot, the way you go at it," he laughed. He remembered with a slight shake of his head and a big smile how impatient Jill had been for the frozen molasses to finally thaw enough to be able to spoon some out. She had even begged until he gouged out a gooey hunk with his hunting knife and they had laughed and laughed as she tried to eat it all in one bite.

"I can't help it, I just crave the stuff. I guess it's because our diet in the cave was usually so plain, you know?"

"Aw, it's alright, Honey, it's just a good thing that our Abe was a health food nut and left all these goodies!" He stood there with his hands on his hips admiring the

219

shelves above the firewood and the large glass and metal containers of wheat germ, granola, dry milk, brewer's yeast, bran, raisins, dried beans, whole wheat, honey, and oh, so much more.

"It's a wonder, that's what it is, Little One," he said, patting her on the head and going to the task of skinning the two rabbits.

"Saved you the livers, Jill," he said, pulling them out of his pocket where he had them wrapped in a clean handkerchief.

"Yum…thanks, Uncle Andy," she said, around a mouthful of goo.

Laughing, he said, "A person would never know that you would not hardly eat liver for nothin' when we lived in the cave!"

Grinning sheepishly, she began to put things away and clear up the table, wiping the sticky residue from her place there.

"How about it if I put on rabbit stew for supper?" she said, thinking to change the subject.

"What?" he spoke with mock severity. "Is food all you can think about?"

"Aww, come on," she laughed, playfully pushing against his massive shoulder. "Go on and tend to the chores, before you stir up trouble, you big old bear!"

"Alright, alright! Some people just like to nag!" he said, as he rushed out the door with a big grin on his face.

"You!" she laughed as she threw the wet rag at the door as it closed. Oh, but it is wonderful to be feeling so good again, she thought, as she moved to feed the fire and prepare to put the stew on to cook. She would put in a cup or two of those dried vegetables and throw in some bran and brewer's yeast. Mmmm, she thought, licking her lips in anticipation.

220

How nice to enjoy eating again, too, she thought. I just don't understand what is happening. How can I be feeling so good with leukemia destroying my body?

In some ways, too, the days were harder now that she was feeling so much better. More and more she thought of her parents and especially Larry, with whom she would have spent her life if this illness had not come upon her like it had. She still loved him deeply and missed him terribly.

"We would have been married by now and living in that little place up the river that we had planned to rent. Why, oh, why Lord? I don't understand all of this," she said aloud as the tears ran down her face. She continued to work on their supper as her thoughts went on.

She had had so much uneasiness in her heart for weeks now and just could not put her finger on the feeling. Was it guilt because she had decided to stay away from them? She truly did not think so, because she knew they had already adjusted to her assumed death by the time she was well enough to really think things through, way back there in the cave. Wiping the tears, she remembered having had quite a bump on the head and had been so faint and weak. It had seemed the right decision to just stay away and not put them through her death again…plus the awful ordeal of watching her slowly suffer and die.

And besides, she truly felt it had been God's will that she faint that night there in the woods during the treasure hunt. After all, had that not happened, Uncle Andy would have never come into her life, and she couldn't imagine not ever having known this wonderful man. And what was even more important, was the fact that she had been able to tell him about the love of Jesus, and now Uncle Andy was a child of God! It was worth that to have gone through anything!

"But Lord, why do I feel so upset and uneasy inside? Please help me to understand what is wrong. I know I will die one day, and I have accepted that. Is it that I don't want to leave Uncle Andy? I do love him so, and I don't want him to be alone. But, Lord, with You he won't be alone anyway. Does it have something to do with the awful things that were happening in Madison? Is it wrong to keep Uncle Andy here so that he can't clear his name with the police? After all, we know they think he is a killer, and we know he isn't. I wonder…"

She moved around the tiny space between the fireplace and the table, and mixed up some cornbread from the ample ingredients on the shelves that were there. The stew was boiling heartily now, and she had the fire banked and the floor swept. Looking around, she thought it would be perfect only if Larry were there with her. Bravely, she blinked back the tears that threatened again, and she finished setting the table. She knew that within an hour the meal would be ready and she certainly looked forward to that. She planted her fisted hands on her hips. "You silly goose," she scolded herself. "Uncle Andy is right! All you can think about is eating!"

She smiled as she settled in the rocker there beside the window. She remembered how she had not had much of an appetite for weeks before the hayride that night. She had felt queasy, had frequent headaches, and that awful dizziness…she shook her head remembering how disquieting those spells were. In fact, she realized it had been many weeks since she had felt that way. That's strange, she thought. But great, too, I'd just as soon never have that again. She was sleeping better than she had for a long time, too. And what a relief that was to her. The nights were so very long when she could not

222

sleep. She was even able to nap in the daytime now. It was the first time she had truly felt rested in ages.

"Thank you, Lord, for helping me to feel so good." She sat in deep thought for many minutes there, not rocking or even looking at anything in particular.

Then, with wonder on her face, and tears pooling in her blue eyes, she reached over and picked up the Bible that lay on the small table beside her. She hugged it to her and said softly, "Lord, could it be possible that You are healing me?"

Chapter 35

The next morning, Jill was up early, having slept fitfully during the night. That was unusual anymore, but she was filled with wonder at her thoughts of the evening before, and had not quite decided what it all meant just yet.

They had already had more delicious granola and whole wheat pancakes with blackstrap molasses for breakfast. Andrew had gone off to check his traps and snares and chop some firewood. Jill had been at the table for quite some time, reading the Scriptures, hoping to find an answer there.

She sat now, with her hands folded under her chin as she thought over all the possibilities. If I am being healed, that means we could go home, one part of her said.

Then another part would counter that Andrew would be accused of murder if he went back, and she would do nothing to harm him. If he knew she was getting well, would he insist that she go back to her family, no matter the risk to his own self? Yes, she thought he would.

So then, did she tell him what she was thinking or not? And what if he did insist they go back, even if he stayed hidden, could she let him go away and never see him again?

The tears sprang immediately to her eyes, as hopes of seeing her family and Larry mingled with the thought of never seeing Uncle Andy again.

She pushed away from the table and restlessly paced around the tiny cabin. Then she fed the fire, dusted the small table and the rocker, and wiped all the window panes on all six windows. Still she felt such uneasiness until she went back to the table and picked up the Bible again.

224

Oh, God, please help me, her heart cried. She began to look through the worn pages, marked with bold lines in many places.

Presently, she began looking through the book of Psalms. When she got to the twenty-eighth chapter, two verses were neatly outlined with a box around them. Verses six and seven read, "Blessed be the Lord, because He hath heard the voice of my supplications. The Lord is my strength and my shield; my heart trusted in Him and I am helped: therefore my heart greatly rejoiceth; and with my song will I praise Him."

Jill felt the tears come to her eyes, and she got up and moved to the front window. Standing there, she re-read the Scriptures and began to feel the peace of God sweeping over her. I will trust in Him, she thought. Lord, I will trust in You. I *will* trust in You!

"Lord, I *will* trust in You," she said aloud as she gazed out the window. Smiling, she wiped her eyes and made the decision to just wait until she felt clear direction from the Lord, and then she would know what to do.

She walked to the window near the wall lamp and idly watched a blue jay that was eating bread crusts she had thrown out for the birds. Then her eyes came upon the Scripture and note burned in the log wall. "May the good Lord bless all who may take refuge in this place."

"Bless good old Abe, Lord," she thought. And seeing the Scripture verse, Deuteronomy 33:27, she recalled the words, "The eternal God is thy refuge and underneath are the everlasting arms."

Smiling, she made an instant decision. She moved swiftly across the room to find a good sharp knife. She may not know how to burn something in wood, but she certainly could carve.

The sharpest knife was a hunting knife with a long curved blade. Oh well, it will do just fine, she

225

thought. She went back to the wall lamp and with a cloth she picked up from a low shelf she carefully dusted the logs where Abe's words were burned and also the two or three logs underneath.

She had to reach quite high, to get at the right angle for carving, so she went back to the woodpile and chose a fat round log that had been split and was flat on one side. She laid it on the floor to give her the height she needed. Gingerly, she stepped up on the log and reached down to the little table for the sharp knife.

Carefully she began to carve, working swiftly lest Uncle Andy should return before she was done. She formed each letter beautifully.

"The Lord is my strength and my shield: my heart trusted in Him and I am helped: therefore my heart greatly rejoiceth; and with my song will I praise Him." She smiled sweetly as she finished the last word.

The Bible on the table beside her was opened to the place, and she was just starting to carve the word "Psalm" when she decided to make it in big bold letters. So she braced her feet and pressed the sharp knife firmly into the log, concentrating on getting it to just a certain depth.

She came to a small hard knot in the log and pressed very hard, still trying to hurry as she could hear Andy at the woodpile now.

Suddenly, she felt her foot slipping on the log and knew she was going to fall. As she tried to catch herself, somehow, the knife viciously slashed across her arm, cutting very deeply, just as she fell.

"Oh!" she cried, as she landed in a heap on the floor. The knife flew away from her, but she hit her head on the corner of the hearth. Everything began to get black and her ears began to roar. Vaguely, she was aware of the sound of Uncle Andy's axe at the woodpile.

226

Chapter 36

A few days later, far away in Madison, the snow fell gently from a gray sullen sky. The air was warmer than it had been for days, and in spite of the snow, there was a smell of spring in the air.

It was afternoon, and there were many gathered at the little church. A special prayer meeting had been called for healing and peace to return to the community.

In the store that morning, a separate and very special prayer time was experienced by several who had been most deeply affected by the events of the fall and winter. Tom, Mary, and Wilma Martin had been there with Larry Miller. His mother Faye and both of his sisters had come along with Jill's parents, Joan and Frank Clark.

The group had begun to have regular prayer times since the day the killer had been caught. Raymond Jay Peters had been the central concern of their prayers. The group had also experienced much compassion and heartache over the story of Raymond's sister, Maybelle, who they had learned had been placed in a special nursing care facility.

This particular day, Widow Watson had decided to come with her daughter-in-law, Annie, in tow. She had had such good visits with Mary Martin recently and the godly love she felt radiating from her friend gave her the strength to allow God to work in her heart toward forgiving her assailant, also. Mary had reminded her that the Scriptures tell us that we must forgive others in order for God to forgive us. She had been sharing about the wonderful peace He had given her and Tom and Wilma after they had truly been able to forgive the man who had murdered the twins. It was so awesome to the Widow Watson, and she had spent many hours talking about it all

227

with Annie, and even more time with her Heavenly Father, who had helped her, through His Word, to finally come to the place where she could completely forgive this Raymond Jay Peters. What was even more amazing was that she found she could even love him.

She was hurt and bewildered, though, that her son, Max, just would not discuss any of the good that was coming out of the situation. She grieved that he seemed to be getting more hard hearted and bitter each day.

So, that morning, she had taken Annie along to the prayer meeting with intentions of having special prayer for her son to be able to forgive and put it all behind him, as she had done.

Old Jack Barnes and Pete Greer had stopped by the store about the time they were deep in prayer. They had found themselves intrigued by the love and caring that filled the room. Old Jack knew of the miracle that forgiveness had brought to the Martin family. Bob and Susan Greyson had been sharing with him, and he had even spent time in prayer with them about this whole situation. Of course Pete knew, too, because his good buddy, Old Jack had shared with him.

And so it was that they had decided to have a special community prayer meeting. Suddenly it seemed urgent that they all come before the Lord together and set things right in their little town again. They knew the mystery was solved and the hows and whys, but they each had to deal with how it had affected their own lives.

The men had decided to go to Pastor Jordan and pray with him and see if it would be the right thing to call a meeting right away, that very afternoon. Somehow, the time seemed to be at hand.

The people who were gathered found themselves in quite a discussion of the events that had led to their coming together.

228

A fellow with a pointed nose and wire-rimmed spectacles, looked over them, raised his eyebrows, and asked indignantly. "Just how can we forgive this Raymond Jay Peters, when he won't even make a full confession?" Sarcastically, he said, "It's like he had a memory loss or something, swearing he doesn't know anything about Jill Clark! Humph! An arrogant person like that doesn't even deserve to be forgiven," he stated emphatically and sat down with a thump, looking all around for people who agreed with him.

Mary Martin took Joan Clark's hand in hers and smiled reassuringly at her as the stinging words rang in the air. Joan's eyes pooled with tears as the murmurs went through the small sanctuary.

"That's right! Did anyone even hear of him wanting to be forgiven? That's what I want to know!"

"But it's not for him that we would forgive, it's for our own hearts," Hannah Edwards stood to her feet. "We didn't deserve to be forgiven or loved by Christ, but He died for us! He loved us and we were *all* sinners!" She paused, taking off her glasses and wiping her eyes with a lace handkerchief.

"You all know that no one has been hurt more than Tom and Mary here. They had two of their family lost because of this man. I happen to know that they have already forgiven him. I think if they can do it, you and I ought to be able to!"

"But I tell you, he don't *deserve to be forgiven!*" It was the grating voice of Bones Jones from the back row. He fairly shouted in his anger.

"You are all wasting your time and this here meeting is just useless! I for one don't even know why any of you would forgive him and *I ain't gonna!*" With that, he stormed out the door and it quietly sucked closed. The silence in the sanctuary was tremendous.

229

After a few long, silent moments, someone began to sing. It was the sweet clear voice of a young girl.

> Oh, how I love Jesus.
> Oh, how I love Jesus.
> Oh, how I love Jesus,
> Because He first loved me.

The silence continued in the room, except for Wilma's voice singing strongly and sweetly. She had risen to her feet. She, who had had two brothers viciously murdered and had gone through her own struggles to find peace in her heart. On she sang:

> To me He is so wonderful, and I love Him.
> To me He is so wonderful, and I love Him.
> To me He is so wonderful, and I love Him,
> Because He first loved me.

People all over the sanctuary sat in silence and found tears coursing down their faces. Then as one, Wilma's parents stood beside her and began to sing along. Right away, Larry and his family joined them, and Widow Watson, along with Annie. Max had not come.

Soon they were all on their feet and some were weeping openly. Jill's parents sobbed in each other's arms.

Bob and Susan Greyson stood arm in arm, tears on their faces, but with a radiant joy as the peace began to flood their souls. Larry's mother moved to the organ and continued to play the song softly in the same key that Wilma was singing.

People began to move toward the Martins and Clarks, and weeping and hugs were mingled together. They could sense that there was victory in Jesus just ahead.

230

At that moment, the sheriff moved to the front of the little chapel and reverently stepped to the podium. There he silently placed a small wooden carving: a likeness of a large man with long hair, a beard, and short pants. Gently, he patted the open Bible that lay there, and with a sob, he turned into the arms of the pastor who stood beside him. Doctor Jamison stood near the back of the church with unshed tears in his eyes and a tremendous struggle in his heart. As he saw the tender gesture of the sheriff's he fell to his knees weeping openly, sobbing from the depths of his being.

He began to cry out to God, praying aloud, and people all over the room prayed with him. The time of forgiveness was indeed at hand for all of them.

Chapter 37

On the edge of town, a very large man stumbled as he walked along, leading a little black horse. Only minutes before, they had finally come to the road, and he had left the deep snow of the woods in great relief. A sudden rush of adrenaline at the ease of travel here had given him new strength even though he had been walking almost continuously for the past twenty-six hours.

He swallowed the last bite of jerky and set forward in grim determination. He knew he walked into unknown terrors of being falsely accused of murder, but that seemed unimportant to him at this moment.

He stepped to the side of the pony, urging him on and looked anxiously at the burden the small horse pulled on the travois. The horse plodded along wearily, but he, too, seemed to know he was near the end of the long journey, and bore his burden with renewed vigor in his step.

The small figure on the travois lay still and the fragile face was so very white against the taut, dark wool blanket. A great lump came up in the huge man's throat as he said softly, "We're almost home, Little One," and he smiled as he saw the slight movement of her head as she acknowledged hearing his tender words.

He shuddered as he recalled the lurch of his heart that day when he had found Jill lying in a great pool of her own blood. He had thought immediately that she was dead.

"Oh, Jill," he moaned in agony as he had rushed to her side. His eyes blurred with tears now, as he remembered seeing the gaping wound in her forearm, and the slowly coagulating blood forming around it. He had applied pressure directly on the wound, and it seemed to be enough to stop the flow of blood, almost cut off by

232

clotting by now. He had sobbed as he grabbed the kettle from the fireplace. He quickly poured scalding water on the needle and thread he kept in a small packet among his things.

Leaving the needle in the cupful of boiling water, he wiped Jill's face with a cool rag, calling her name, and weeping openly.

"Oh, Dear God, don't let her die now, not after all we've been through together. And she's been getting well, I know she has!" His prayers and cries of anguish intermingled as he ministered to the unconscious girl. He carefully sewed the wound together, pouring alcohol liberally over everything. He was so very thankful that she was not awake as the pain would have been unbearable. And, again, he was thankful to Abe for the alcohol and for having thought of nearly everything they had needed since coming to the log cabin.

He did not try to move her until he had her arm carefully and neatly bandaged and was certain that the bleeding had stopped.

As he gently carried her to the bed, she seemed to weigh nothing in his massive arms. "She's so tiny, and yet so important to me, God. Please, please don't let her die," he prayed fervently, as the tears made tracks down into his beard.

All that night he had bathed her face and prayed over her occasionally placing a spoonful of warm broth between her lips. By reflex, she swallowed the tiny sips as he raised her head to take them. Soon after he had begun to lift her head, he had found the hard knot on the back. After closer examination, he saw that it was not an open wound, but he started wrapping snow in cloths and keeping them against the lump on her head. It had already gone down in size by the time she began to stir, sometime before morning.

Again, the tears were close, as Andrew remembered his tremendous relief as she woke up. He had been so fearful that she never would.

That had been several days ago, and he shook off the feeling of fear that crept into his very being as the thought of losing her. No matter if it meant her anger or not, he was taking her back to civilization so that she could be properly cared for. "That's just the way it is," he thought, walking even faster in his determination. He was sorry it upset her so much to have him bring her back and he knew it was only her concern for him that made her not want to go home.

He had been wondering if she was in some kind of remission. He had read about that sort of thing in the medical column in his stacks of newspapers in the cave. What if it were possible to have a remission for many years with proper care? He would not know how to give her the care she might need to survive more than a few short months. He just could not bear the thought of being the cause of an earlier death for her.

They had talked this all over in the few days before they left the small cabin. They both shared their fears for the welfare of the other, but fortunately for him, he thought with a grim smile, he was the biggest after all, and finally she had given in, with much weeping.

They had prayed together before leaving the cabin, and he had written a note and cleaned the place for the next occupant, or Abe, whichever came first. They both had experienced deep remorse at leaving the snug little cabin, where they had found such joy together and in their Lord. They even left the treasured Bible there on the little table where they had first found it. Perhaps some other traveler would find answers for his life in the worn pages of the precious Word of God.

Andrew had finished carving the Scripture verse below the words Jill had carved already. "I *will* trust the Lord," he'd said quietly. "I have to…"

In the final hours at the cabin, Andrew began to feel a sense of urgency to get Jill to medical care. She just was not rallying like he had hoped and prayed she would. Evidently, she had lost far too much blood. He cringed now, as he walked along, recalling the great pool he had scraped and scrubbed the morning after she had awakened. Still there was a faint stain there on the rough floor where she had fallen.

"Uncle Andy?" He heard her call weakly from the travois. "I'm here, honey," he said, as he stopped the horse and knelt beside her.

"Are you alright?" he asked with concern furrowing his brow, as he brushed the hair from her face.

"Oh, yes, I'm feeling much better! Where are we? I slept for so long and I was dreaming that I was in church, Uncle Andy. The singing was so beautiful." She smiled sweetly up at him, and then he saw her face take on a puzzled expression.

"But Uncle," she said, turning her head from side to side, "I can still hear the singing." Then, looking at him, she asked, "Can you hear it, too?"

He looked around, and realized for the first time that, yes, there was definitely singing in the air. He must have been so lost in thought that he simply did not notice before.

"Well, yes, Little One, we are in Madison now, and the singing seems to be coming from the little church up there," he said, gazing up the snow-packed road. The snow had stopped falling now, leaving a thin soft dusting over everything.

"Oh, please, Uncle Andy, can we go there?" She raised herself up on her elbow, trying to peer in the direction of the beautiful singing.

"You could just leave me in front of the church. I'm sure there will be someone in there who would take me home and that way you could go away and no one would ever have to see you. Could we do it that way, please, Uncle?" She placed her small gloved hand on his arm and pleaded with her eyes.

"We will go to the church, Little One, but I'm not leaving you. I will stay with you for as long as they will let me and that's that!" He started to rise and smiled reassuringly at her.

"But, Uncle," she began.

He placed a large finger on her lips and said gently, "You must remember that, with Christ I can do all things, just like the Bible says, and He will help me through it all, even if I spend the rest of my life in prison. The most important thing to me now is to take care of *you*."

She quietly shook her head and settled back on the travois as he stumbled to the horse's head and took the reins.

"Come on fella, we're almost there," he said wearily.

Jill was concerned about her great loving friend. He was so tired, and she feared for his health as much as he did hers. But she had not been able to convince him to rest at all since leaving the little log cabin, and she did not know what he might have to endure before he was able to get any rest at all.

The tears began to pour down her pale face as she thought about him and then she found herself anticipating the reunion with those she loved.

236

They were outside the small church now, and the singing that poured from the place was ethereal. My, they sound like angels, she thought. She closed her eyes and listened as Andrew stood beside her, seeming to know that it wasn't quite time to go in.

> Walking in sunlight, all of my journey;
> Over the mountains, through the deep vale.
> Jesus has said, 'I'll never forsake thee.'
> Promise divine that never can fail.
> Heavenly sunlight, Heavenly sunlight,
> Flooding my soul with glory divine;
> Hallelujah! I am rejoicing,
> Singing His praises, Jesus is mine."

Without even a break in the singing, someone started to sing another song and the congregation of believers inside the church joined right in.

> What a friend we have in Jesus,
> All our sins and griefs to bear;
> What a privilege to carry,
> Everything to God in prayer.
> O, what peace we often forfeit,
> O what needless pain we bear,
> All because we do not carry
> Everything to God in prayer."

As they continued to sing that beautiful old hymn, Jill motioned to Andy that she was ready to go inside. With tears on both of their faces, they prayed together there under the big oak, as he held her like a babe in arms. Then, taking a deep breath, he started up the stone steps of the church, cradling her close to his heart.

The door quietly sucked closed behind them, and they stood there in the back of the sanctuary in awe of the very presence of God that seemed to fill the place.

Andrew felt the weakness in his legs as he stood immobile, and felt that his knees were losing their strength. He knew fatigue was about to overtake him, so he moved to take the few steps to the back pew so that he could set Jill down there.

As the movement caught the eye of the doctor who was near the door, he looked in disbelief at the giant of a man standing there with the small young woman held in his arms. He could not see her face as her back was to him, but his doctor's practiced eye saw immediately that the black-haired, bearded man was in some kind of distress. Automatically, he moved toward him and was able to take Jill from the big man's arms just as he slumped to the floor. As he did he looked full into the girl's face and recognizing her, he said in wonder, "Dear, sweet Jesus!"

The singing came to a stop as folks all over the sanctuary became aware of something happening in the back of the room. They were all standing, and not everyone could see. Some began to whisper and the words were passed in hushed tones throughout the congregation.

"It's Jill! She's alive…"

"How can this be?"

"Who is that man?"

"What's wrong with him?"

Then, as Jill's name came resounding to their ears, her parents looked bewilderedly at one another, and at Larry, who stood with them.

"Can it be?" Jill's mother tried in vain to peer around the people who crowded toward the rear of the room. Her husband firmly took her arm, and they made their way through the people. Suddenly, as one, the people began to step aside to let them pass, wonder on each face, and breathless anticipation in every beating, throbbing heart.

The first voice they heard that was not a whisper was that of their beloved daughter. They looked at each other in wonder, as they knew for certain that it was her.

"Oh, please, someone help him!" Jill pleaded, tears coursing down her face. Old Jack was on his knees beside the man, rubbing the backs of his hands awkwardly. Pete had rushed to find a glass of water and get a wet paper towel from the restroom.

Old Jack looked up into the face of Jill as the doctor held her. "Who is he?" he asked her.

"Oh," she said, "he is the dearest friend I ever had in my life. His name is Andrew Pazak. Is he alright?" she anxiously scanned the faces of the people in the crowd. The first loved one she saw was her mother, Joan.

"Mama! Ohhh, Mama!" She fell into their arms as her parents took her from the bewildered doctor. He moved quickly to the side of the fallen man, and in minutes he was able to tell the people that the man seemed to have collapsed from exhaustion.

Pete Greer stood transfixed as the doctor and Old Jack worked over the big man there on the floor. He seemed unaware of the new commotion in the sanctuary as people began to rejoice that Jill had been returned to them.

She awkwardly hugged each one with her one good arm and they sobbed against her shoulders and neck until she was fairly drenched with their tears. She had never experienced such pure joy as that of looking again and again into the faces of her parents and of the one she loved more than life, her beloved, dear Larry. She could not get enough of looking at him. Dearest Larry, with tears on his face and love there in his eyes that was beyond all she had ever dreamed possible. He would forgive her for leaving, she knew he would. Oh, how glad she was to be home.

***

Her eyes traveled around the familiar sanctuary, and took in every detail of the beloved place of worship where she had grown up. Then her eyes rested on a small dark object on the altar. So familiar, but she could not see it clearly from the back of the sanctuary.

It seemed to draw her, and she tried to rise from the pew where she sat. Those around her saw her eyes on the altar and assumed she wanted to go there to pray, so tenderly they aided her wobbly steps up to the front of the church.

She stood there, with puzzlement on her face as she stared at her little wooden carving of Uncle Andy.

"What? How…" She turned to her daddy who stood beside her, supporting her firmly. "How did my carving get here? I thought it was lost."

"Your carving, Honey? You must be mistaken. This is the carving that was made by the killer. You know, Jill, the one who killed the twins?" The lump in his throat made him unable to continue.

"So much has happened since you have been gone," Joan declared. "Oh, Jill, we all thought that he had killed you, too!" Her mother burst into anguished yet joyous tears as she threw her arms around the confused girl.

"But, thank the Lord, he has been caught and we can go on with life. In fact, that is why we are here today, Jill. To pray for the killer and to try and get our lives back

240

together." The pastor said, as he placed his hand on her shoulder. He could see the confusion in her face.

"But that *is* my carving," Jill stated flatly. "I made it of Uncle Andy months ago, and it was lost. I don't know where. I can't understand how it got here."

Suddenly, the sheriff, who was standing quietly nearby, realized what she was saying. It *was* a likeness of her friend there. He does resemble the killer, Raymond Jay Peters, he thought. This is very strange.

Suddenly, sucking in a ragged breath, Jill turned and looked at the pastor. Deeply into his eyes, she searched for the truth. "Pastor, did you say *the killer has been caught?*"

"Why, yes, dear. It's all over now."

Jill began to sob as the reality hit her. They wouldn't accuse Uncle Andy after all! He was cleared of the whole awful mess. She squeezed her eyes shut…"Oh, thank you Father," she prayed. "Thank you!"

"You see, we thought…" And through her tears Jill began to tell those around her of the fears they had had about returning to Madison.

Only Old Jack noticed Pete Greer sitting beside the big man on the floor, with tears coursing down his face. Someone had placed a pew cushion under his head and someone else had covered his huge frame with an overcoat. The man slept peacefully there on the floor as though it were the most comfortable feather bed in history.

"Andrew, my boy, I can't believe it's really you. Dear God, how could this be? All these years…where have you been boy? You were alive all this time and I never knew. Dear God in Heaven, how can it be?" Pete sat muttering and crying as Old Jack sat nearby on the end of a pew, listening, trying to make some sense out of what all this meant.

241

Well, he decided, the pieces would all be neatly fitted together in time. He just knew that, from somewhere deep in his being, a miracle had happened here today. "Many miracles, he thought, as he rose to his feet and moved to the side of his friend sitting there on the floor. Silently, he put his hand on his shoulder. There was no need to say anything. He just wanted Pete to know that he was there. He wanted to enjoy the peace he felt deep inside himself, and rest in the Glory of an All-Knowing God.

Epilogue

A year later, at springtime, Bob Greyson sat at the kitchen table with his friend Old Jack, as his wife Susan moved around the kitchen making coffee.

"I saw Larry and Jill today," Susan said, with a smile. "They are so happy since the wedding last Christmas. Jill invited me to come up to their little cabin by the river and teach her how to knit," she continued, as she poured the steaming coffee into their mugs.

"Mom?" Randy said as he came rushing into the house, with his fishing pole in tow. "Some of us guys are going fishing, okay?" He glanced at the two at the table and stood there with a sheepish grin.

"You could go too, if ya want," he said, looking into Old Jack's lined face. It had been a long winter and both knew they had a wondrous summer of their favorite pastime ahead.

"Aww, you fellas go on without me, this time. I'll go another time, huh?" He gingerly sipped the hot coffee and winked over the cup at Bob.

"Besides, Old Jack and me, we've got some plans of our own, don't we, friend?" Bob said with a grin. They had taken up playing dominoes with Pete Greer and Andrew Pazak and were looking forward to at least a couple of games before chore time.

Andrew lived with Pete now, and the two were inseparable. It had been such unexpected joy two days after Andy's return to Madison that he awoke to find he was in the home of his long lost friend. It was obvious to him now that there was only one body in the grave back by the little cabin near the huge pine, and Pete was delighted to know the youngster had not died in that fire after all! Andrew had made a speedy recovery, and after finding that Jill had been quickly revived with a blood transfusion and was doing well, he had cried many tears of sheer relief.

In a few days everyone knew how Jill had thought herself to be dying of leukemia. They knew how she and Andy had reveled at the news that she was not dying. Everyone had rejoiced for her speedy recovery with proper treatment for anemia.

Andy and Jill had smiled knowingly in their gratefulness to Abe when the doctor announced that all those good foods found at the cabin had evidently been instrumental in her near recovery before the fall. Her arm had healed nicely, and Andy had been commended again and again for his quick thinking and skill when he stitched up the wound.

"Bob, will you take this coffee cake by the Widow Watson's on your way to Pete's? You know how Maybelle loves it." She stopped wiping the counter top and, gazing out the window, she thought of the crippled little woman who now lived with the Widow, and what joy she had brought to their community this past winter.

She fairly radiated with the love of Christ and never tired of telling how He had brought her through the darkest despair of her life. She faithfully told how one day, she believed He would break through that barrier and save her brother, Raymond Jay, also. She wrote to him every day, and she and the Widow Watson drove down to the prison at least once a month for a visit. Each time they went, they took at least one other person from Madison, and they all felt that, undoubtedly, the Lord was working in his heart and that one day, Raymond Jay Peters would find himself becoming a child of God, too.

As Susan stood there, she saw her daughter, June, walking along with her friend Wilma. They carried baskets of wild strawberries and were laughing gaily together. They called something cheerily to Randy as he rushed away.

Susan took a deep breath and smiled as she went about the task of wrapping the foil around the coffee cake. Suddenly, she heard Husky barking, and glancing again out the window, she saw Jerry Davis and his little niece horseback riding along the roadside. Susan smiled; glad to see that her family was visiting Uncle Jerry and her horse again. Bonnie fairly beamed with pride as she waved and called happily to the girls walking in the meadow. She reached down then and patted the dear little black pony she loved so much.

As Bob and Old Jack walked off down the road a few minutes later, Susan stood in the doorway of their little cabin. These are probably the happiest days of our lives, she thought, as she had done before.

"I think I will go up the hill for a walk up by the stream. It has been a long, long time," she said as she reached for her jacket and stepped down from the porch. Stretching her arms toward the sky, she breathed deeply of the clean fresh air and shook her hair loose.

"All's well, and God is on the throne," she declared joyously, gazing up at the blessed blue sky.

"What did you say, Mother?" June asked as she came around the corner of the cabin with Wilma.

"Oh, nothing really," she said with a grin, as she turned toward the bubbly stream. "See you later. I'm going for a walk up the hill. You girls have fun." She could hear the birds singing as she leisurely strolled away, humming her own tune.

The End

About the Author

Jane Priest Wilson is a Christian author who has been writing seriously since high school. She was a columnist and feature writer for two newspapers, and has written ministry newsletters for more than twenty-four years. Jane also has numerous *works in progress* including a second novel. There are stories about deaf children and other children's stories, a children's chapter book, among various other writing projects.

Jane and husband John are also writing about their experiences in various ministries through the years since 1988. Stories about things like the day they saw a woman killed at a post office, the true story of "The Machete Brothers", and the summer they sang gospel music and conducted Sunday services in a café. That was in the Yukon, on the Alaska Highway. There are also many tales to relate about pastoring churches, ministering in dozens of nursing homes, and while on the road as music evangelists, which is what they are currently doing. They began their travels in a converted school bus years ago. Having seven flat tires in one trip was not fun! There are good and bad things that happen along the way, and inspiring one-on-one experiences that are worth sharing with others.

John and Jane married as high school sweethearts forty-six years ago. She is thankful that he has been a tremendous encouragement to her in her writing. They raised their two awesome children, Jimmy and Lara, and now have four wonderful grandchildren! Their family and serving the Lord are their greatest joys in life.

Miracle in Madison, Jane's first novel, was begun in 1978, when they were dreaming of moving to the woods and living off the land. They were looking for peace and tranquility in their lives. Ten years later, their dream had come true in the woods of Minnesota and they had found that peace through the Lord Jesus Christ. The book was finished just before starting in the ministry in 1988. Of course, after giving her life totally to Jesus Christ, it was re-written to make this mystery book into an "inspirational suspense novel". It is their earnest prayer that you will draw closer to the living God through the telling of this tale.

There will be a sequel coming out in the future.
Watch for _Miracle on the Mountain_!

Made in the USA
Charleston, SC
28 September 2012